BECOMING
MUHAMMAD ALI

BECOMING MUHAMMAD ALI

A NOVEL

JAMES PATTERSON AND **KWAME ALEXANDER**

Illustrated by Dawud Anyabwile

JIMMY PATTERSON BOOKS
LITTLE, BROWN AND COMPANY
NEW YORK BOSTON LONDON

HOUGHTON MIFFLIN HARCOURT
BOSTON NEW YORK

JIMMY Patterson Books / Little, Brown and Company
Hachette Book Group
1290 Avenue of the Americas, New York, NY 10104
JamesPatterson.com

Houghton Mifflin Harcourt
3 Park Avenue, 19th Floor
New York, NY 10016
hmhbooks.com

First Edition: October 2020

JIMMY Patterson Books is an imprint of Little, Brown and Company,
a division of Hachette Book Group, Inc. The Little, Brown name and logo are trademarks
of Hachette Book Group, Inc. The JIMMY Patterson Books® name
and logo are trademarks of JBP Business, LLC.

Houghton Mifflin Harcourt Books for Young Readers is an imprint of
Houghton Mifflin Harcourt Publishing Company

The publishers are not responsible for websites (or their content)
that are not owned by the publishers.

The Hachette Speakers Bureau provides a wide range of authors for speaking events.
To find out more, go to hachettespeakersbureau.com
or call (866) 376-6591.

The Library of Congress Cataloging-in-Publication data is on file.
ISBN: 978-0-316-49816-6 hardcover
ISBN: 978-0-316-70348-2 international edition

10 9 8 7 6 5 4 3 2 1

LSC-C

Printed in the United States of America

The wonders and woes
in this novel are true . . .
or based on truth
and real things . . .
that happened
to real people . . .
or real people
we imagined . . .
to be true . . .
for real.

ROUND ONE

I remember *everything*. You probably would have too. That night was a piece of American history.

The Clay family phone was dusky black with a rotary dial, and it sat on a wooden table in the neat-as-a-pin living room of the little house on Grand Avenue in Louisville, Kentucky.

Some twenty of us were crammed like sardines into the room, waiting for that phone to ring.

Waiting. Waiting. Waiting for Cassius to call home.

It was a February night in 1958. And I remember it like it was *yesterday*.

My best friend, Cassius, was three hundred miles north in Chicago, and that night he was fighting for a championship in the Golden Gloves boxing tournament.

Cassius wasn't a professional yet, just an amateur. Tall, but a little skinny, and a lot raw. Only sixteen years old, like me.

I'm Lucius, by the way. Nice to meet you. You can call me Lucky. All my friends do.

Cassius had already won plenty of bouts all over Kentucky. But the Chicago Golden Gloves was the big time.

When he won there—and we all knew he would —it would be lights out! From now on, people everywhere would know the name Cassius Clay.

And so we waited for the phone to ring.

I remember that living room was so packed with family and friends and neighbors that we could hardly move! The smell of roast chicken and sweet potato pie and cheese grits mixed with the smell of paint and turpentine. Mr. Clay, Cassius's dad, who everybody called *Cash,* was a sign and billboard painter, and he kept his work supplies right there in the house.

"Mrs. Clay!" somebody called out. "When that boy of yours gets famous, he ought to buy you a bigger house!"

"Oh, you know he will!" she answered. Then she looked right at me. "Isn't that right, Lucius?"

"Yes, ma'am, you know it is. Cassius promised you a big house!"

I remember that Mrs. Clay was too nervous to eat. But she wasn't too nervous to talk about how proud she was!

"My Cassius did everything early!" she was saying to a group of ladies. "He crawled early, talked early, walked early—walked on his *toes* like a dancer."

The ladies all laughed—as if they hadn't heard that story a hundred times before. But Mrs. Clay just couldn't help it. Cassius always told her he was bound to be the greatest—with a capital *G*—and she believed it with all her heart.

So did I.

So did everybody in Louisville's West End.

C'mon, phone. Ring, phone, ring-a-ding-ding.

The men and boys around the room—including Cassius's little brother, Rudy—looked at one another with big grins and made punching motions with their fists. The big fight should be over by now. Under those bright lights in the middle of that huge Chicago Stadium, Cassius would be standing tall in the ring with one hand over his head like always—his opponent next to him with head bowed down in defeat.

Then the phone rang.

It was Cassius with news about the fight. And he told it like only Cassius could tell a story . . .

Before the Fight

a reporter asked me
if I thought
I was as good
as Joe Louis
or Sugar Ray was
at my age
and I told him,
I don't think
I'm as good,
I'M BETTER.
Got more FLOW   5
than Joe,
more SLAY
than Ray.
I'm sweeter,
stronger,
and faster.
As a matter of fact,
I'm so fast
                    I can't even catch
                                        MYSELF.

Cassius Clay vs. Alex Watt

FEBRUARY 24, 1958

Here's how it all went down:

The bell rang
in Chicago Stadium
and I could barely see
the lightweight rush me
through the rank cigar smoke
that filled the arena.

6

In the first round,
he threw punches
like pitches,
fast and straight,
striking air
and striking out.

So, I played *peek-a-boo*
in the second,
sending quick jabs
to his head.

You ain't ready for Cassius, I whispered.

Then I shook him up
with a left
and took him down hard
in the third.

He sho' wasn't ready.
But neither was I,
when I found out
who I was fighting
next.

Cassius Clay vs. Francis Turley

FEBRUARY 25, 1958

Frank Turley
was a cowboy
from Montana,
meaner-looking
than an angry ox,
with fists
even meaner.

They said
he broke a guy's nose
with a left jab,
then smiled
when the joker
went tumbling
outta the ring,
blood spurting
everywhichaway.

I'ma lick you good, boss, he said,
winking at me

before the bell rang, and
I believed
that he believed
he would.

Knockout

We traded punches
like baseball cards.

Him, a wild mustang.
Me, a Louisville slugger.

Back and forth,
left and right,

rough
and rugged, till

he cornered me
with two lucky shots

to the jaw
that felt like kicks

from a mule
and sent me tumbling

to the mat, wondering
if I should just stay there.

Long Count

One . . .

While I lay there,
the referee standing
over me, counting
to ten
to see if I could get up,
I wished my father
was sitting ringside
shouting my name.

Two . . .

I thought about home,
about 3302 Grand Avenue,
and playing football
in the backyard
with Rudy, and

Three . . .

the Montgomery kids next door
and who was gonna babysit them
now that I was a boxer,

Four . . .

and whether Lucky
bought the new Superman
like he promised.

Five . . .

I thought about
my granddaddy Herman's story
about Tom the Slave.

12   *Six* . . .

I thought about
how boxing
was gonna set me free,
set us all free, and

Seven . . .

what I'd ask Momma Bird
to cook
for my celebration
dinner
after I got up and

Eight . . .

whupped this cowboy
from Montana
and advanced
to the semi-finals
of the 1958 Golden Gloves Championship.

Celebration Dinner Menu

Two orders of veal
Three slices of white bread
A bowl of cornbread dressing
One large green salad
A bowl of chili
Scrambled eggs
Cheese grits
Baked chicken with baked potato
Two pieces of pecan pie
Five scoops of strawberry ice cream, and
A great big ol' glass
of OJ.

I Jumped Up On

Nine . . .

and Frank kept swinging
like a lumberjack
trying to knock down
a tree
but I kept standing,
kept sticking,
kept moving
like a mighty wind
till the final bell rang
and the judges
unanimously called out
my name
for the win.

Cassius Clay vs. Kent Green

FEBRUARY 26, 1958: GOLDEN GLOVES SEMIFINALS

I was a little weary
from hanging out
the night before
but that didn't shake
my confidence
when I stepped
into the ring,
gliding like a bomber jet
and launching punches
like missiles.

Thing was, Kent Green
was a tank
and he just brushed off
my attack
like you would
a pesky fly
at a picnic.

The evening newspaper read:

The sixteen-year-old pugilist
from Louisville

17

with his quick feet
and a loud mouth
showed promise
in his first two fights
but got outboxed
by the older,
more seasoned,
hard-punching
Kent Green.

On the Phone with Lucky

I might have lost
but I'm still boss.
I lost my stride
but not my pride.
I'm still here, and yeah,
I'm comin' home

but this dream I got
is set in stone:

To be the best
in the hemisphere.
To win the Golden Gloves
next year.

How do I know?

'Cause Cassius is courageous,
tenacious,
and one day
he'll be
the greatest.

You hear that, Lucky?

I'm coming home.

ROUND TWO

Maybe he *didn't* win the Golden Gloves championship in Chicago that year — but my friend Cassius was still bound for greatness. He just *knew* it. And I knew it too. To tell the truth, I think losing that last fight made him work even harder. Made him *focus*. Nobody could focus like Cassius Clay. He didn't let anything stand in his way. Not even a bottle of soda.

Me, I *loved* soda — especially ice-cold in frosty bottles on those hot Louisville summer nights. So did most kids. It tasted soooo good! But Cassius never *touched* it. Not a single sip. "Sugar and acid ain't good for you, Lucky," he said. And that was that.

Focus.

For Cassius, there was no smoking either ("Ain't gonna put that stuff in my lungs!"). And he always went to bed at ten o'clock, even on Saturday nights. Like he wanted to grow in his sleep.

Focus.

After school, we went everywhere together, the two of us. And whenever we headed downtown, we stuck together tight. *Tight like glue.* And we kept our eyes wide open. Because going downtown meant crossing over into the white world. And in that world, four eyes were definitely better than two.

All over Louisville, we saw signs that Cassius's daddy had painted. But the white people who owned the stores under those signs stared at us when we passed by—like they were just waiting for us to do something wrong, or say something fresh, or take something we didn't pay for.

One day, we passed a bicycle store. There was a line of bikes out front, with bright chrome fenders and front wheels all turned to one side. At the end, one bike stood out past the others. It was a brand-new Schwinn Black Phantom, with white sidewall tires, pinstripes, and sparkly paint. It was the coolest bike either of us had ever seen.

Cassius gave out a low whistle when he saw it.

"Look at that bike, Lucky!" he said. "*That's* the kind of bike I should be riding!"

Cassius reached out and stroked the handlebars like he was petting a cat. The chrome gleamed between his fingers.

Then we heard the bike-shop door open. The owner and his wife stood in the doorway, halfway out, at the top of the cement steps. We froze.

"You boys don't want nothin' with that bike," said the man, his face all red and puffy. He started to come down the steps at us, but his wife put a hand on his arm. She seemed a little softer, but still strong enough to stop him. She had reddish-blond hair and a green dress.

"Scoot, now," she said. "You boys get on home."

She knew exactly where home was.

Home meant the West End—mostly black Louisville. It was one of the few parts of the city where the Clays and my folks could buy a house. In most parts of town, they couldn't get a loan to buy a house, couldn't even walk into most hotels or diners. *Whites Only,* the signs said. When Mrs. Clay took Cassius downtown as a kid, he got confused because nobody there looked like him.

"Momma Bird," Cassius would ask, "what did they do with all the colored people?"

One day when Cassius was little, he stood outside the five-and-dime store crying because he was thirsty. When Mrs. Clay went inside to ask for a drink of water, the store guard made her leave.

"If we serve Negroes in here, we lose our jobs," the guard told her. So Cassius went home thirsty, mad the whole way. Cassius was so young, his momma thought he wouldn't remember that day.

But he did.

Granddaddy Herman's Living Room

was always like church
to me.

I was the congregation.
His couch, my pew.

The rhythm and blues on his radio
was the choir, and

Ebony magazine
was his bible.

His sermons were sometimes poems,
other times stories

from history—his and America's.
But my granddaddy's sermons always ended

the same way:
Know who you are, Cassius.

And whose you are.
Know where you going

and where you from.
Amen. Amen. Amen.

Where I'm From

I am from black Cadillacs,
from plastic-covered sofas
in tiny pink houses.
I am from the one bathroom
we all shared
and the living room
you stayed out of.

I am from Friday fried fish
and chocolate birthday cakes,
from Levy Brothers' slacks
and shiny white shoes,
from Cash and Bird,
from storytellers
and good looks,
from don't say you can't
till you try.

I'm from the Kentucky Derby
and the land of baseball bats,
from the two Cassius Clays before me — one
black, one white.
I am from slavery
to freedom,

from the West End
to Smoketown,
from the unfulfilled dreams
of my father
to the hallelujah hopes
of my momma.

My Momma

smells like vanilla,
is always smiling,
loves cooking,
and I bet could make
a whole Sunday outfit
outta needle and thread.

Odessa "Bird" Clay may be
the smallest
of the Clays,
but her heart is the biggest,
wide as the sea.
And when she sings
at Mount Zion Baptist,
her voice is like water,
soft and sweet
as a hummingbird.

She Says the Day I Was Born

my head
was too big
to come out
on its own,
so the doctors yanked me
with some sharp tongs
that left a small, square bruise
on my cheek.

She says I hurt so much
that I cried
and hollered
most of the night
and into the next day,
which got the other
babies in the ward
screaming too,
but probably I was
sounding a rallying cry
to all my little soldiers
for all the brown babies
in the world
to stand up
and be counted.

After That

I vowed to never
let anyone put a mark
on my pretty face

again.

Cassius Clay vs. Odessa "Bird" Clay

MARCH 14, 1943

My first knockout punch
came at the age of one, when
I accidentally

hit my beautiful
momma in the mouth and knocked
her front tooth clean out.

When Bird Gets Mad

at me about something
I done wrong,
she calls me *CASSIUS MARCELLUS CLAY JR.,*
but mostly I'm just *Gee-Gee*
'cause she says
before I could even crawl
I was running my mouth,
and the first sound I made
was the letter *G,* twice,
but probably I was just dreaming
aloud, foreshadowing
my fate,
trying to voice
my future
as a Golden Gloves
champion.

My Brother, Rudy

came two years after
me, and ever since, we've been
like two golden stars

in the northern skies—
inseparable—and our
parents' brightest hope.

Now, My Daddy

Cassius Marcellus Clay Sr.,
better known
around Louisville
as *Cash*,
is the opposite
of Bird.

He's six feet
of bronze
and brawn, and
when he isn't singing
or scolding
or dancing
or joking
with his Saturday night buddies
way into Sunday morning,
he's painting masterpieces — old Bible scenes
on church walls,
new billboards, and signs
on storefront windows — and happy
the whole time.

Signs My Father Painted

Open Lunch and Dinner
Dreamland Bar & Soul Food Café
Our Own Community Delicatessen
Best Charcoal Ribs in Louisville
Parking Around Back
Whiskey by the Drink
Serving Fresh Ice Cream
Colored Waiting Room
This Way for Fun—Fontaine Ferry Park
Whites Only
Segregation Is Immoral
There's No Way Like the American Way
Vote for Progress
We Cut Heads
Percy's Barbershop
Now Buy Victory Bonds
Rock and Roll Sold Here
Closed on Sundays

Some Sundays

when Papa Cash would stumble in
after being out
all night,
Momma would ask him
when he was gonna fix
the wobbly front porch
or the leak
in the roof,
and he'd ignore her
or start fussin',
then leave back
out the house
with me and Rudy
tagging right along,
over to Granddaddy Herman's house,
who would give us
something sweet,
like Black Jack Taffy,
show us magic tricks,
tell us funny
and not-so-funny stories
about famous
and not-so-famous Negroes,
bounce us

on his one good knee,
all while smoking a cigar
and arguing
with my daddy
till they both fell asleep.

Growing Up

When Rudy could walk
we got a pet chicken,
a dog named Rusty,
and a new house
with a brand-new backyard
near the size of a basketball court,
where we would play with Rusty,
and chase
the chicken
and each other
around.

We had a goldfish pond
that I watched Daddy build,
plus a vegetable garden
with snap beans
that I loved
to peel,
and onions
that I loved to eat,
raw.

Everything

was easygoing
and laid-back
on our side
in the West End,
where we lived,
so that's where
we played
and prayed
and went to school
and grew up
but every now and then
we'd cross a line
and wonder
why we couldn't stay
and play
on the other side
of it.

The Other Side

When Rudy got old enough
for Bird to let me
take him
out and about,
we ran,
jumped, and
played on every inch
of Chickasaw Park,
'cause it was in our neighborhood
but we'd never been
to Fontaine Ferry Park
even though
it had
amusement rides
and even though
it was right next to our neighborhood.

We were gonna go
to Fontaine
and dare anybody
to stop us.

We told Momma
we were walking over

to Granddaddy Herman's
to help him
chop some wood,
which was true, but first
we were gonna cross the line
and go have some fun
at Fontaine Park.

The *Whites Only* sign
met us at the fence
outside the park
and the two police officers
with Colt 45 pistols
made sure
we stayed there.

Later That Day

we chopped wood
in silence
and when we were done
Granddaddy Herman preached
a sermon
that I'll never forget.

Two Louisvilles

For a Negro boy
in the West End,
you know you can
play tag
in Chickasaw Park
but you better not be caught dead
in Shawnee Park
or Boone Square.

And, no matter how many times
you hear the crackle
of wooden roller-coasters,
smell the hot buttered popcorn,
and watch thousands
of happy white kids
eat cotton candy,
you know you're not allowed
in Fontaine.

Boys, there's two Louisvilles:

One where you go school shopping
for clothes

and one where you can't
try on the clothes
beforehand
or bring 'em back
if they don't fit.

One where you roller-skate
outside your house

and one where you're not allowed
inside the local rink.

One where you can go
to some movie theaters

and one where you have to
sit in the balcony
and barely hear
the movie.

One where you got a decent job
with decent pay

and one where you get a raise
but your house payment goes up.

One where you can go
to the amusement park
with your friends

and one where you stand
outside the fence
like a caged bird
singing the summertime blues,
because your skin
is like a crow — black
and unwelcome.

One for whites

and one for blacks.

Know who you are, boys.
And whose you are.
Know where you going
and where you from.
Amen. Amen. Amen.

I Want to Be Rich

I said to
Rudy as we lay
in the backyard
under the stars
talking to the chicken
and each other
about being famous
one day like
Chuck Berry,
that way they'd have to
let us in
their amusement park.

But, since neither one of us
could sing or dance,
and we both loved
to slap-box,
we figured maybe we could
be rich like
Joe Louis instead,
buy the darn park,
and build
the first American Cadillac roller coaster,
candy-apple red,

so that any kid
could get into Clay Park
and ride the rides.

Momma Hollered

from the kitchen,
interrupting
our moonlit dreams and
big ideas.

Gee-Gee, time for you
and Rudy
to wash up,
say your prayers,
and go to bed.

I liked pranks,
so I stood up,
told Rudy,
DON'T MOVE!
There's a great
big ol' copperhead snake
in the grass
next to your head,
and he jumped up,
screaming
all the way into next week,

forgetting all about
Fontaine Ferry Park.

But I never did.

ROUND THREE

Did I mention I always wanted to be a writer? Maybe you guessed, since you're reading this. Written by Lucky. Or I guess I should say, by Lucius Wakely. Sounds more writerly. But luck definitely played a part in me becoming a writer.

Because I was lucky enough to know Cassius Marcellus Clay Jr.

Cassius would be the first to admit that he didn't like to write—or study. He showed me his report card once. His average grade was 72, which was just about passing. He got a 93 in metalwork, though. I guess you could say he was good with his hands.

I was different. I *liked* school. In fact, I bawled like a baby if I didn't get 100 on a test. But Cassius wouldn't let me cry about stuff like that.

"Dry it up, Lucky!" he said. "School ain't life."

Once I got a B on an English essay, and I knew it wasn't fair. Cassius made me walk right up to the teacher after class and argue with him. I went back and forth with that teacher for a half-hour—but in the end, I got my A.

"You got it 'cause you deserved it," said Cassius, "and 'cause you didn't back down."

Cassius didn't like to read much either, but he really liked being read to. Sometimes we'd sit together in his front yard with his little brother, Rudy, and I'd read from newspapers or magazines or comic books. Especially Superman comics. Cassius loved Superman. *Loved* him! He loved that Superman was stronger than everybody else. He loved that he was world-famous. He loved that he defeated villains and that people called him a hero. "Truth, justice, and the American way." That was Superman's motto. Cassius loved that part the most!

There were times, growing up in Louisville, when Cassius was my own *personal* superman. One day, the three of us—me, Rudy, and Cassius—were walking down the street when a car rolled right up next to us. It was so close, I could hear the radio and smell the cigarette smoke inside. The car was filled with young men. White men. And I guess they thought we were on a street we shouldn't be on.

The man in the front passenger seat leaned out the window. "This ain't your neighborhood," he said. "You boys are in the wrong place." Then he flashed a knife —a switchblade.

I was really scared. So was Rudy. Maybe Cassius was, too. But he didn't show it. He stepped right out in front of me and Rudy.

"You dumb enough to try something with that knife?" Cassius said. He looked right at the guy, staring him down. *Daring* him.

It was hot that day. The temperature inside that car must have been triple digits. The guys were getting mad because we weren't moving. We were just standing there. I saw the guy with the knife say something to the driver. The car engine stopped. Then all four car doors opened at once.

Cassius turned to me and Rudy. "Time to go," he said. Cassius was brave, but he wasn't stupid.

All we heard was "Hey!" as we started running. With his strong legs, Cassius could have been home sitting on his porch before Rudy and I got to the end of the block, but he slowed down so we could keep up. There was no way he was going to leave us behind.

My Friends

Everybody's
got a nickname
on our block.

Rudy is sometimes *Hollywood*
on account of Daddy
named him
after one of his favorite movie stars:
Rudy Valentino.

My best friend, Ronnie, is *Riney,*
'cause that's how his grandmother
screams it
from her living room window
when the streetlights start flickering:
RINEYYYYYY!!!

Lucius is *Lucky,*
on account of
one summer he fell
through a plate-glass window
and not a scratch was on him,
then the next summer

he crashed his bike
into a parked car
and flew over the car
into a bed of hay
in the back
of a passing
pickup truck.

We call Corky Butler *Chalky,*
but not to his ashy face, 'cause
he's strong
as a mountain lion,
meaner-looking
than a jackal,
and he gives out
black eyes — to boys
and some men, too — like candy
on Halloween.

We got Jake and his brother, *Newboy,*
who both sing doo-wop
in a group called
the Blue Tones.

There's two *Bubbas* — one short, one tall.

Big Head Paul's got a head
big as a battleship.

Cobb, aka *Lil' Man,* is two years older
and two feet shorter, but
got a real job
and new clothes,
new shoes,
and a bank account to prove it.

When they see me coming,
it's always, *We should call Gee-Gee
the black Superman.*

Faster Than a Speeding Bullet

We shoot marbles,
play touch football
in the backyard,
stickball out front
in the street,
hide-and-seek
with the girls,
see who can spit
the farthest,
pretend
we're Jack Johnson
knocking out
the Great White Hope,
and run races in Chickasaw Park,
but my favorite game
is when Rudy
throws rocks
at me
and misses
'cause I *duck*
so fast
I make him call me *Donald,*

jump so high
I can nearly touch the sky
and grab a cloud.

It's a bird, it's a plane . . .

Card Trick

You got some speed on you, Cassius,
Granddaddy Herman says
after we finish pulling weeds
from his garden.

He shuffles the deck of cards,
then tells me
to pick one.
You remind me of myself running bases.
How good were you at baseball? I ask,
pulling the king of hearts
and sliding it back
so he can't see it.

Better than most, he answers,
throwing the cards
all over his kitchen table.
As good as Jackie Robinson? I ask.

Coulda been.
Really?

Coulda been as good as Cool Papa Bell, Josh Gibson, and
all them other players you ought to know about too.

Did they play in the major leagues?
You writing a book, or what? he says, shaking
his head
and telling me
to pick the cards up.

Conversation with Granddaddy Herman

Shouldn't you head home with your brother?
He's got to do homework. Momma Bird stays
on him.

*What about you in school? Your lesson's important, ya
know.*
I know. I get by, I say, handing him the cards
back.

That ain't enough, Cassius. "Life ain't no crystal stair."
What's that mean?

*It means, you gotta work twice as hard to get half as far
as the rest of these folks out here.*
Can I ask you a question, Granddaddy?

I don't know, can ya?
Why'd y'all name me and my daddy after a
slave owner?

*Boy, you got some learning to do, about baseball and
your name.*
. . .

*The o-riginal Cassius Marcellus Clay wasn't no slave
owner. In fact, he freed all his slaves on the Clay plantation, including your great-granddaddy, my father.
Then he went and fought for the Union in the war.
You and your daddy's named after a man with prin-
ciples, probably the only white man I ever knew to be
good. Know who you are, Cassius, and whose you are,
understand?*
Yes, sir.

*Now, I know you hungry, 'cause you always eating, so go
ahead and get some of my cookies, and leave me three.*

Thank you, Granddaddy.

Get a glass of milk, too, so you can get on home.
I can stay a little longer, if you need help
around here.

I got stuff to do, boy.
. . .

*Tell you what, while you eating up all my snacks, I'll
tell you the story of Tom the Slave, and then you get on
home. Deal?*

But what about my card?

You mean the king of hearts you're sitting on? he says,
smiling.

. . .

That Same Night

at bedtime
I tell Rudy
about how Tom the Slave
escaped to freedom
by hiding in a casket
on a ship
of dead bodies
on its way
to London, England,
and how when he got there
he became a famous
bare-knuckle boxer
who would've won
the heavyweight championship
of the world
if a hundred Brits
hadn't gotten so mad
that he was beating
their fighter
that they rushed the ring
in the ninth round,
clobbered Tom,
and broke
six of his fingers.

That ain't true.
You calling Granddaddy Herman a liar,
Rudy?

I'm just saying, you think it's a real story?
Probably, I don't know. It's a good one, at
least.

Why didn't he fight with gloves on?
You writing a book, or what?

. . .

Rudy, before we go to sleep, pick a card.

Ritual

I practiced
card tricks
every night
on Rudy,
even stayed up
long after he fell asleep,
trying to find
the right card,
trying to prove
to myself
that I was smart
at something.

One Friday

after school,
me and Riney and Rudy
were outrunning
the city bus
heading home,
figured we'd save
the ten-cent fare
for some Finger Snaps
at Goldberg's,
when I took a detour
and told 'em,
Hey, let's go
to that hamburger joint
over on Broadway.

We sat in Rainbow,
splitting two cheeseburgers
and fries,
me joking about
Riney's bald spots
from the terrible haircut
his grandmomma
gave him, and
Rudy winking at every girl

that walked by
with her momma,
when in walked Tall Bubba,
who we hadn't seen
since the accident.

The Accident

We were playing ball
on Virginia Avenue,
our block against theirs.
It was me and Riney, Short Bubba,
and Lucky against
Cobb, Big Head Paul, Jake,
and Tall Bubba.

Rudy was still sick
with the chickenpox bad,
even though our neighbor told us
we could cure him
by flying a chicken
over his head.

Cobb's block always beat us
'cause Big Head Paul
was a three-sport legend
in the West End.
I mean, he could
hit a rock with a pencil.
And Tall Bubba, from Smoketown,
had arms so long
he could probably box

with God.
He caught everything.

But then Cobb pitched me a fastball
that I cracked so high
it went way over
Tall Bubba's outstretched arms
and landed inches
from the storm drain
near the corner of 36th and Virginia,
where it slowly rolled in
before he could grab it.

Tall Bubba was the only one
with arms long enough
to reach down the drain,
so he did, and no sooner
than he screamed, *I GOT IT, FELLAS,*
it blew up
right in his face.

We used to smell gas
all the time around there,
but none of us ever figured
it was anything
that mattered.

We Never Saw Him After That

until we sat in Rainbow,
splitting two cheeseburgers
and fries,
telling jokes,
winking at every girl
that walked by
with her momma.

Until today.

Conversation with Tall Bubba

Hey, Bubba.
Hey, Gee-Gee.

The fellas are over there.
Yeah, I see 'em.

. . .
. . .

They fixed the gas leak.
That's good.

I heard the City's gonna pay you for what happened.
Naw, they ain't even calling my daddy back.

That ain't right.
. . .

When you coming back to school?
*I been doing school at home. Teachers come to
my house. Don't wanna be seen looking like this.*

You still cool as a pool to me, Bubba.

I look kinda ragged and old with no hair and a
busted-up face.

A little mature, maybe. You still Tall Bubba, though,
still too slick for tricks.
Thanks, Gee-Gee. Hey, what did you get on your
report card?

How'm I supposed to know that? Report cards don't
come out till next week.
Naw, they came out today.

They did?
Yep! I'll see ya around.

Report Card Friday

I GOTTA GO, I hollered
to the fellas.
Gotta get home
and get the mail before
my daddy does.

Riney sat there laughing at us
and finishing the rest
of the juicy cheeseburgers
with pickles and loads
of ketchup
by himself.
See, he'd been signing
his own report cards
since first grade
'cause his grandparents
couldn't read
so well anymore.

But my parents could.
C'MON, RUDY, LET'S SPLIT!

School

Big Head Paul was
the smartest of us all.
His hand was always
the first
to go up
when a teacher asked
a question
about trees
or bees
or oceans and seas.
Science was his thing.

Riney always brought
peaches and pears
from his grandmomma's backyard
for our teachers,
so whether he studied
or not, he always got
decent grades
and even made
the honor roll once.

Lucky was what you might call
a natural genius.

He knew a little bit
about everything
and loved to talk
as much as I did,
but his claim to fame
was he could spell
mostly any word
in the English language
and he could read
real fast,
which came in handy,
'cause I couldn't do
either very well.

In the Second Grade

we were sitting
in circle time
taking turns
reading *Fun with Dick and Jane*
and it was my turn
and I swear the *F*
in *Fun*
turned upside down,
started floating
off the page,
and then
some of the other letters
inside the book
started playing
ring-around-the-rosy
and switching their order—*Jane said, "Run"*
became
Rane "said" Jun—and
that didn't sound like
it made sense,
so I didn't say it,
then the *F* came back
but it was dancing around so much
that I started getting dizzy

and my stomach hurt
and some of the kids
started calling me dumb
and I almost threw up
right there in the middle
of second grade circle time,
so now
I just try
to memorize
what I hear
and make up
what I don't.

Failed Plan

I ran home so fast
I could see my big toe
starting to bust out
of my shoe
like an inmate
in a prison.

Rudy was two blocks
behind me,
so when he finally walked up,
winded and holding
his chest
like he was gonna collapse
in our front yard
from running
so fast and far,
I was sitting on the porch
scared straight
'cause OUR mailbox
was empty.

Conversation with Momma Bird

Gee-Gee, come in here.

. . .

I thought you were supposed to be trying harder.
I did. I understand everything we're doing in
school, mostly. It's just sometimes—

*Don't make excuses, Cassius. Your father won't like this
at all. You know that!*
I know.

*They gonna fail you, you keep getting these kinds of
grades.*
I'm not gonna fail. Grades don't make the
man, the man makes the grade.

*Double talk not gonna make them stop thinking you
dumb, Gee-Gee.*
You think I'm dumb, Momma?

Course not. I'm just hoping you know you not.
Momma, I came in this world smart and
pretty, and I'm gonna leave it the same way.

*Well, this weekend we gonna go see Miz Alberta Jones,
see if she can help you out with some of your subjects.*
Yes, ma'am.

Now go on and finish your chores before dinner.
Momma, I'm too old for chores. Rudy's the
youngest, he should—

*Gee-Gee, am I too old to cook dinner and wash your
dirty drawers?*
Uh, no, ma'am.

*Then neither are you. Now, you best stop yappin' and
get your skin thickened up, 'cause your daddy'll be home
soon, and he's gonna hit the roof when he sees that report
card.*

. . .

Turning Point

Daddy came in the house
not like he usually did—flirting
with Bird
and talking all loud—no, this time
the storm door shut,
and he came
in the house, slow
like a preacher
walking to the pulpit
to deliver a funeral eulogy.
I heard him drop his art tools
at the door,
then heard Momma's footsteps
as she made her way to him.

Rudy and I sat at the dinner table.
Me, not sure how long his hollering
was gonna be
when he saw my grades,
Rudy sneaking a bite
of the cornbread
from his plate.

When we finally saw his head
peek around the corner,
like he was looking in a coffin
afraid to see what was there,
he motioned for us to get up,
so we did.

Boys, a giant tree has fallen, is all he said,
hugging us like
he'd never done before.

I Was Twelve

when I was so fast
I could dodge rocks
and snatch a fly
outta midair

when Rudy caught
chickenpox, and
Tall Bubba lost
his face
chasing a tennis ball

when I almost failed
outta Madison Junior High
and decided I was gonna
make a lot of money
so my children wouldn't have
to watch the world
from behind a fence

when I learned how to
shuffle a deck of cards
with one hand
and make the king
of hearts

appear
in the other.

I was twelve
when my daddy came home
and told us
that Granddaddy Herman was,
God rest his soul,
dead.

ROUND FOUR

We were all just kids, doing the dumb stuff kids do. But Cassius was always different, with those big eyes on some picture show that the rest of us couldn't quite see. We all dreamed about the future. But I think Cassius really, truly *saw* it. Like a movie. Starring *him*. And he always did things his way.

93

I remember mornings when the bus would stop to pick us up for school. Everybody got on except Cassius. He'd hang back and let the bus get a little head start, and then he'd race it all the way to school—twenty blocks down Chestnut Street—with the rest of the kids hanging out the windows and cheering him on. Especially the girls. "Crazy Cassius," they said. "He's as nutty as he can be." Those same girls were the ones who winked and waved at him when they saw him shadowboxing after school, throwing punches at himself against a brick wall. Whatever he did, he seemed to attract attention. Like a star.

But there were times when he was silent and thoughtful, too. Some nights, me and Cassius and Rudy would just lie on the grass out in back of their house, looking up at the sky. Cassius would say he was waiting for an angel to appear. Rudy always had his momma's Kodak Brownie camera handy. He didn't want to miss a chance at getting the world's very first angel snapshot. I was never sure what Cassius wanted from that angel. Maybe he wanted the angel to tell him that he really was the greatest, or give him some kind of heavenly blessing. Maybe he was looking for a sign that there was a higher power watching over him. Anyway, it never happened. We never saw a single angel on Grand Avenue. But before too long, Cassius found some inspiration right down the road.

At the racetrack.

Back then, we all lived pretty close to Churchill Downs, where they hold the Kentucky Derby every year. It was one of the classiest and fanciest places in all of Louisville. Still is. It's where the best and fastest horses in the world train. Cassius *loved* the horses —the way they looked, the way they moved, the proud and noble way they held their heads. But he wasn't content to just watch them. He wanted to *race* them. So he would go out to the track in the morning, while the dew was still on the grass. When the trainers brought out the horses for their exercise, Cassius would run right alongside them. "They're the only thing faster than me!" he'd say. One time he actually got in front of a horse on the track. When the horse swerved to get out of his way, the rider fell off and landed hard on the dirt. *Bam!* That was the end of Cassius's horseracing career. After that little incident, he got kicked off the track for good. But he still hung around the stables. He couldn't get enough of those thoroughbreds. Most of all, he loved the shape of their smooth, powerful muscles, and he wanted to get his own body in condition like that —stronger and faster than anybody in the world.

During the Summers

we went to
Camp Sky High,
played paddleball
with wooden rackets,
and pulled pranks
on unsuspecting counselors.

We shot hoops
with a tennis ball,
and tried
not to get pushed
in the pond.

When we got home,
we played roller-skate hockey
on 34th Street, but
that got boring,
so Rudy and I made scooters
out of our skates.

On Friday nights,
we had fish fries, and
on Saturdays, everybody on the block
went to Riney's,

sat on his lawn,
and watched
boxing fights
on an old TV
that his grandmomma
set outside
on her front stoop.

Tomorrow's Champion

At seven o'clock
each Saturday night,
fathers, sons, and
a few daughters sat
in awe
for three televised fights,
spellbound by the rhythm,
by the hustle,
by the might
of two stroppy boys
throwing wild blows
till one went down
or the bell rang
at the end
of the third round
and the judges decided
who was *Tomorrow's Champion.*

Fifty Cents

Bird didn't like me
and Rudy betting
on account of God
not liking ugly,
And all gambling is ugly, Gee-Gee, but
I liked taking
Riney's money, so
when it was time
for the Saturday Night Main Event,
I bet him that
swift-footed Gorgeous George
was gonna knock out Billy Goode,
which he did,
then I collected
my winnings,
gave Rudy a quarter,
and spent the rest of the night
dreaming
of being in the ring one day,
and trying not
to make eyes
at this short cutie
named Tina Clark,

aka Teenie,
who all my friends said
was in love
with me.

On the Way Home I Would

skip
and duck
like I saw the boxers
do on TV

tell Rudy to hold
his hands up
so I could punch them
like I saw the boxers
do on TV

make up songs
that rhymed
in my head
and dance
between the cracks
on the sidewalk
like I was in a ring,
like I was Gorgeous George,
like I was a bigtime boxer

on TV.

Odd Jobs

Everybody had a job.

We all wanted bikes,
shiny, new ones.
So we saved our money
from birthdays
and Christmas
and odd jobs.

Most of the fellas
would skate around
white Parkland
delivering roses, tulips,
and other colorful flowers
for Miz Kinslow's florist shop.

Riney used to cut grass,
fifty cents for the front,
seventy-five for the back,
'cause the back was always larger.

Me and Rudy delivered
Ebony magazine
every month,

but my regular pay came
from babysitting
the Montgomery kids,
which was
the easiest,
'cause all we did was listen
to boxing matches
on their big tube radio.

Cobb got his bike first,
two in fact—one for his cousin—'cause
he was shining
one of his customers'
wing-tipped mahogany shoes
at the horse track
down at the Fairgrounds
for forty cents, and
the guy refused
to pay him, tossed him
a race ticket instead,
for a long-shot horse named
Getouttamyway,
that ended up winning,
paying Cobb
a whopping
five hundred

and sixty spanking dollars.

Riney never got a bike,
'cause his lawnmower skills
were as bad as his
grandmomma's haircutting skills.

I made enough money for a bike,
but as it turned out,
I never had to spend it
on one.

And here's why . . .

The Block

Riney and Lucky
were shooting marbles
on the curb.

Jake and Newboy were singing
"Under the Boardwalk"
on the front porch.

Rudy was across the street
talking to a girl
from the sidewalk

'cause her daddy didn't let
no boys in their yard.
I was shadowboxing

next to the redbud tree
in our yard
and Short Bubba

was telling everybody
that Cobb said
that Big Head Paul told him

that he saw Chalky
pulling a boxcar.
With. His. Teeth.

The Legend of Corky Butler

Chalky was
the biggest,
strongest,
meanest
kid
in Louisville.

He lived
on the other side
of the railroad tracks,
in Smoketown,
he had fists
the size of grapefruits,
and he used them
to pummel
anybody who stepped
into the ring with him,
and to terrorize
everybody
in the neighborhood.

He didn't ride a motorcycle
but always had on a biker's jacket.
He was sixteen

or twenty-six,
nobody really knew,
but he looked like a man
and was built
like a truck,
which he would lift to
impress the girls.

When he wasn't bullying
or knocking out dudes
in the ring
or on the street,
we used to see him
hanging out
at Dreamland,
where all the gangsters hung.

So, if Short Bubba said
Cobb said
Big Head Paul said
Chalky pulled a car
with his teeth,
he probably did.

The Story Continues

So, while Short Bubba's telling us
the story,
Teenie and some of her friends
walked by,
stopping in front of
the Montgomery house
next door,
posing and posturing
in matching yellow skirts,
dancing and singing,
stealing glimpses at me,
and pretending
like they weren't impressed
with me stabbing the air
like my fists were knives.

All the fellas followed
behind them like puppy dogs,
but not me, I stayed back
throwing jabs
at the wind
till my father drives up
in his rusty black pickup,

and rolls down
the window.

Conversation with My Daddy

Hop in here, Gee-Gee, he says.
Yes, sir. Hey, Rudy, I scream, c'mon!

Just me and you, Cassius. Rudy can stay here.
Where we going? I ask, climbing in the front
seat.

We going where we going, that's where we going.
. . .

. . .
Daddy, can I ask you something?

Boy, I don't know, can ya?
It's just—

Speak ya mind, boy.
For Christmas, can I, uh, get a pair of boxing
gloves?

. . .
Daddy?

You want to be successful, Cassius?

Yessir.

*Education is the bicycle that'll get you there, Cassius. You
keep pedaling, sometimes uphill, sometimes down.*
Huh?

*I wanna see you doing better in your schooling, not
throwing punches at the wind.*
Just having fun, Daddy.

*'Cause for every one you see in that ring, a hundred been
knocked out. Of life.*
. . .

You gotta work on them grades.
I know.

*Your great-granddaddy was a slave. Your granddaddy
was in jail. I ain't finished high school. You got the
chance to be the first Clay to really do something.*
Not if you include the white Cassius Clay
that I was named after. He was a lawyer and a
soldier. Granddaddy Herman told me he was
a hero who freed all his slaves.

He didn't free all of 'em. What does that tell ya?

Maybe he wasn't a hero.

Gee-Gee, I want you to be the first of US to go to college.
Do something with yourself.
School's not for me, Daddy. I'm gonna be a
star, just don't know how I'm gonna shine yet.

Education is the only way I know how to find your shine,
son.
You found yours.

I would always draw since before I could walk. When
I got to paint in grade school, everything changed. A
teacher showed me the great Sistine Chapel in a book and
I decided that was the kind of art for me.
So, you were always gonna be an artist?

Until I run up on Jim Crow, who said Negroes can't
be artists. So I did the next best thing and did signs for
pawnbrokers and preachers.

. . .

All the Clays got natural talents. Your granddaddy, rest
in peace, coulda played big leagues, but they didn't allow
no black players.
I know.

This world is white, Cassius, he says, pulling up to a church. *This world is snow white.*
What we doing here? We going to Bible study or something?

Just come on. Something I wanna show you.
. . .

Angels

We walk into
Clifton Street Baptist Church
and sit
in the third row
of the pews
like Sunday service
is about to start,
only it's Tuesday
and church is empty
'cept for me, him,
and a whole bunch
of flying ladies
wrapped in white sheets
with green wings
holding flowers
painted on
the ceiling.

Whatchu think of my latest masterpiece, Gee-Gee?
This is your Sistine Chapel, Daddy?

Well, I ain't no Michelangelo, but it's decent work.
It's the same as the picture from the Bible,
right?

Similar. I added my own style to it.
It's real good, Daddy, but I got one question.

Say it, then.
Where were all the black angels when they
took the picture?

When We Pull Up

in front of our pink house
all the neighborhood kids
are still outside
joking and
jump roping and
playing tug o' war
with the setting sun.

I climb
out of the blue-black truck
ready to finish sparring
till nightfall
when Daddy slams
his door and hollers,
Get that tree
and my painting stuff
out the back, Gee-Gee.

Early Christmas

Lying under
the tarp
that covers
our Christmas tree:
    his vinyl primer
    his lettering brushes
    his lettering enamel
    his cups and pencils
    his erasers and rulers
    his stencils
    his crusty buckets
    his brush cleaner
    his chalk powder
    his ocean-blue glass paint
    his burnt-umber acrylic paint
    his mineral oil
    his wobbly old ladder
and MY
BRAND-NEW
FIRE ENGINE–RED
SUPER-JUMBO JET
SPEED-RACING
SCHWINN BICYCLE.

All Hail the King

Everybody stood
at attention,
eyes glued
on me
and my super bike
like I was Commander Cassius,
the Leader of Louisville.

I let Rudy ride first
but all he did was fall
and scrape my brand-new chrome,
so I promise to teach him
later.

I let Riney
take it for a quick spin,
then I hopped on, rode around
the block
four times,
and had Cobb time me,
since he was the only one of us
with a watch.

On my last trip,
Teenie strolled over,
her lips shooting me
a smile big as the sky,
her teeth white as clouds,
then she took her keys
off her purple rabbit-foot key chain,
hooked it
to the spotlight clamp
on my handlebars,
and said, *For good luck, Gee-Gee,*
so you don't fall,
so I let her ride
on the handlebars
up and down
the block twice,
then I rode
the night wind
by myself,
popping wheelies
and showing off
my smooth-as-butter
fire-engine royal-red
Schwinn bike
with its shiny spotlight
crowning the front.

After School Started Back Up

in the fall,
Teenie didn't come around
as much
and when she did
her eyes didn't light up
like stars
no more,
which was okay with me
'cause between
runnin' with Rudy,
getting tutored by Miz Alberta,
and cruising
around town
on my Schwinn,
I didn't have time
for much else.

Mystery

One day
I was flying home
with Rudy
on the handlebars
trying
to outride
the dusk
and get home
before the streetlights
came on
when I swore
I saw Corky Butler
running from
the alley
behind our house.

The lights
on my bike
worked like
the hot water
in our tub — sometimes.
Today, they didn't,
so we hustled

in the near dark,
hoping we could sneak in
the back
before Daddy stumbled
through the front,
when *BAM!*
we hit
something
and Rudy and I went flying
onto the gravel.

We got up, bruised,
inches from
what was not a *something*
but a *someone*
lying stone-cold dead
on the gravel.

We ran inside,
both of us wondering
to ourselves
who the body belonged to,
whether it was really dead,
and neither of us saying
a single word

to each other
or anyone else
about it
ever.

ROUND FIVE

Growing up, Cassius couldn't understand why white people had it better than black people. It didn't make any sense to him. He knew they weren't any better than black folk, just different.

But whenever he asked his momma about it, she'd get real quiet and tell him to be careful. She told us that there were things you could say in the house that you couldn't say outside. And there were ways we could act around other black folk that we couldn't act around white people. Even how we walked, how we talked, and who we looked at. It sounds crazy, but it was true. We had to be one way for ourselves and another way for the rest of the world. We couldn't let white people see what we really thought or how much we really knew. It was the only way to stay safe. Mrs. Clay told us other things, too.

She told us that back in the days of slavery, plantation owners would kill the smartest slaves, because they knew they were the most dangerous. I knew I was smart. But maybe deep inside, that's why I didn't want to show it. Maybe I didn't want to look dangerous.

Cassius didn't buy any of it. Said he didn't care, that he was always gonna be Cassius Clay, no matter where he was, or who he was with.

When I got to seventh grade, my momma made me apply for a scholarship to the Catholic school across town. It was where all the smartest kids went. When I got the letter saying that I'd won the scholarship, I cried. Sad tears, not happy. I told my mother I didn't want to go. I didn't want to be one of those kids. Too dangerous.

But when Cassius heard about it, he wouldn't let me cry. He said, "Lucky, don't you ever be afraid of being smart. Don't be afraid of *anything!*" And on the first day I came out of my house in my new Catholic school uniform, Cassius was right there on the sidewalk waiting. He walked me all the way to school to make sure nobody bothered me. Then he ran all the way back to his own school. He was probably late. But he didn't care. "That's what friends do," he said. And Cassius was always a great friend.

Looking back, I remember that *everybody* liked Cassius. Most teachers liked him because he was quiet and polite. "Never gave me any trouble," said Mrs. Lauderdale, his English teacher. And outside of class, he was really funny — always cracking jokes and breaking us up. Cassius was like a magnet. You wanted to be around him. But I don't think anybody knew him the way I did. Nobody else really knew what was behind that big smile and loud laugh. I saw the *serious* part of Cassius — the part of him that was determined to go places, be someone special, and make a mark in the world that would last forever. He was gonna make the world notice him.

Back then, in the 1950s, boys didn't talk about loving their friends — especially guy friends. But Cassius did. One night when we were sitting on his front steps watching fireflies, Cassius told me he loved me because I understood him. Today, he'd probably say, "Lucky, you really *get* me." And I did. I was proud of it. I still am.

The Day I Was Born Again

It was a Friday,
hotter than noon
on the 4th of July.

The one fan we had
was blowing
on Momma,
who was sitting
in the living room
reading the Bible,
probably praying
that Daddy would stop
galivanting
like he did
most Friday nights
till Saturday morning.

Sitting on the porch,
showing my
latest card trick
to Lucky
and showing off
my new white Chuck Taylors,

the heat
was punching
me in the face,
and the sweat dripped
like a waterfall.

I couldn't take it
no more, so
we hopped on our bikes,
Rudy got on
my handlebars,
and we took off
chasing
the breeze
and my destiny.

134

We Stopped In

Aunt Coretta's bakery
on Virginia Avenue,
split a sweet pecan honey bun.

Rode by Percy's barbershop,
saw Cobb
through the window
in the chair.

Passed the downtown YMCA
on 10th and Chestnut,
heard the loud projector
coming from the backyard.

Bulleted past two gangsters scrapping,
one with a knife, outside
of Dreamland nightclub.

Rode by Louisville Gardens,
home to Cardinals Basketball.

Cruised Fourth Street,
hollering and laughing
to the moon

like we owned the world,
when the heavens opened up,
reminding us

that we didn't.

The Thunderstorm

emptied so fast, it
was like somebody unzipped
the sky onto us.

Shelter

So the three of us
drop our bikes
outside
Columbia Auditorium,
then dodge
a million raindrops
as we run up
its fourteen stairs
to escape
the monsoon.

The first two things
we see inside
are:

Thousands of folks
checking out the latest home
and kitchen gadgets
on display at the annual
Louisville Defender Expo

and

Chalky, aka Corky Butler.

Crazy Eyes

Corky Butler didn't
so much walk
as he did lumber
in our direction,
clearing his path
like a grizzly bear
on his hairy toes.

He was in
a dingy, too-tight
warm-up suit with
tattered black Chuck Taylors
covering his paws
that he probably bullied
some kid
half his size for.

When he got to us,
he stepped
on my sneaks,
and bumped Lucky
with just enough force
to make him lose
his balance

and knock Rudy backwards
like a domino
into an old couple
checking out
a Hoover vacuum cleaner.

Then he stopped,
his dusty-looking face
so close to me
I could see the gumline
of his gigantic gray teeth,
could smell
the stream of sweat
crawling down
his dull, bald head.

Corky closed
his mouth,
curled up his crusty lip,
lifted his chin
like he was studying me,
so I balled my fists
in my pockets
just in case
this was a test.

Nice sneakers, he said,

then, before walking out

the front doors,

he pointed

his two stubby

V-sign fingers

at his eyes

and mine.

I got my eyes on you, Cassius. Corky Butler's

watching you.

After

he left
we roamed the Expo
tasting samples
and not talking
about what happened
even though
we were all thinking
the same thing—I might have to
fight him someday—when
I ran into
Teenie Clark again
while waiting
for Rudy
to come out
the bathroom.

Before That

Rudy said he felt
like throwing up,
so we ran
to the toilet.

Before that
we ate too much
Kentucky peanut brittle.

Before that
we said hello to Miz Alberta,
who was teaching people
how to vote
on a cardboard voting machine that
all the kids
in our neighborhood
helped her build
last summer.

Before that
I told Gorgeous George,
You may be gorgeous
but I'm pretty,
which made him laugh,

then come at me with,
Kid, you may be pretty
but I'm exquisite,
resplendent,
an ivory knockout.
I'm so beautiful
I should kiss myself,
and then he closed his eyes
and poked his lips out,
which made EVERYONE laugh.

Before that
we waited in line
for almost thirty minutes
to get an autograph
from the boxer
and sometimes wrestler
Gorgeous George.

Before that
Lucky pretended
he was blowing a saxophone
while we listened to
Billie Holiday sing
"Too Marvelous for Words."

Before that
we marveled
at the mahogany record player
spinning "Lady Sings the Blues"
at the RCA booth.

Before that
me, Lucky, and Rudy shared two bags
of toffee popcorn.

Before that
I saw Teenie
eating popcorn
and talking
to Miz Alberta.

Before that
we stood drenched
in the front
of the auditorium,
patting ourselves dry
with paper towels

and right before that
Corky had just stepped

on my sneakers
and walked out
the front door
when Teenie Clark
passed by me
with her parents
and her little brother.

Conversation with Teenie

Hey, Gee-Gee.
Hey.

Whatchu doing?
Rudy ate too much brittle, I said, pointing
toward the bathroom.

Oh.
. . .

How's your jet-plane bike?
Still good.

*I can't wait for school to be over. I'm going to camp.
Gonna play tennis and swim and whatnot. What you
doing this summer?*
Nothing, I don't know.

Cassius, you don't like me.
What you mean?

*What I mean is you never have words for me. Always
"Yup" and "I don't know" and "Oh . . . Uh"!*
Oh . . . Uh.

See, I swear you can be so aloof.
I don't know what that means, Teenie, but it
doesn't sound polite to me.

Cassius, everybody knows I like you.
I like you, I mean, you're nice and all.

Just nice?
I don't know.

How about agile?
Huh?

*As in quick. You don't know, Cassius? I'm the fastest run-
ner in our school.*
The fastest girl, maybe.

I could outrace you.
You're dreaming, Teenie Clark.

If I'm dreaming, then bet me.
You don't want no parts of me, Teenie. I'll run
circles around you. I'm so fast that last night
I turned off the light switch in my bedroom
and I got in bed before the room was dark.

*You may be funny, but won't be no laughing when I
outrace you.*
Name the date and the time, and meet me on
the line. You may be fine, but I'm faster than
an airline.

How about now?
It's raining now.

You scared you might melt?
NAW!

*Then get your buddies, and meet me outside. I'm gonna
catch my stride, and you gonna lose your pride. Poor
Gee-Gee.*
It's on, Teenie Clark.

Bet.
Bet.

Shock

When we get
to the front door
Teenie's momma
comes running up behind us
and pulling her
by the arm
while her daddy
shoots us a
You all better get
'fore I get you look,
so we do,
flying out the door,
back under
the night rain
to get our bikes
to go home,
but MINE
ISN'T THERE.

Tragedy

This year . . .

The last new episode of Rudy's favorite show,
The Lone Ranger, aired on the radio. And he cried.

We had to hide under desks with books over our
heads because the principal said the Russians had a
hydrogen bomb.

80 million locusts swarmed the desert in
French Algeria.

An earthquake struck Southern California.
Hurricane Hazel hit North Carolina.
And the University of Kentucky wouldn't let
Cobb's older brother, Arthur,
the best running back
in the state of Kentucky,
play for their school
'cause of the color
of his skin.

There's been natural disasters and wars,
all kinds of human failings and tragedies,

but right now
none of it feels
lousier
than my royal-red and white
Schwinn Cruiser Deluxe
with chrome rims
not being
where I left it.

The sixty-dollar bike
my daddy bought me
isn't there.

It's GONE
like *The Lone Ranger*
and somebody STOLE it.

Lucky Said

he saw a security guard,
so after I ran
around in the rain,
crying and
hunting
for the thief,
we went back inside Columbia
to report the crime
but the guard
was too busy eating peanut brittle
and flirting with every lady
that walked by
to care about my misfortune,
so we just asked him
if there was a real cop
anywhere around,
and that's when he pointed
downstairs.

Downstairs

was a basement
with a gym
that smelled

like a boys' locker room
with no ventilation

like a hot, musty day
after rain

like cut grass
in August

like the sweat
of a dozen boys
after hours
doing pull-ups,
skipping rope,
and hammering away
at heavy bags
and each other.

Columbia Boxing Gym

The plastered floor
was coming apart,
the fluorescent lights
barely hung from the ceiling.

The grimy, white-brick walls
were covered
in Louis and Dempsey posters and
large red signs

with gym rules,
training checklists,
Tomorrow's Champion announcements,
and corny

but uplifting quotes
printed on them:
Winners are not those
who never fail.

They are those
who never quit.
The place was loud.

Old men coaching kids—some

I knew,
some I didn't,
some white,
most black—guys

lacing gloves
and talking trash
about what they were gonna do
to each other

in the ring,
and, thing was, it felt good,
real good,
to be in there.

In the Middle

of the gym
was the square ring
with the ropes
I'd only seen
on TV,
and two muscly teenagers
I knew
from school
throwing wild punches
at each other's heads
and missing.

On the punching bag
was a tall fella
with a lighting-fast blast
of a blow
that looked like
it could tear a man's head
straight off his neck.

Egging him on,
occasionally looking
around the gym
at the goings on

was an old white guy
with two ballpoints in his pocket,
hair only on the sides
of his head,
and cuffed black pants so baggy
you could barely see his shoes.
When he saw me,
he walked my way.

Conversation with an Old White Guy

You lost, kid?
No, sir, but my bike is.

How'd you lose a bike?
SOMEBODY STOLE IT, AND I AIM TO
FIND OUT WHO!

Simmer down, now.
WHEN I FIND HIM, I'M GONNA
WHUP HIM GOOD, TOO.

*Not a good idea to tell a policeman you gonna commit
assault.*
You the cop?

Twenty-five years.
Can I file a report or something?

You see the culprit? Any witnesses?
No, sir. But I think I know who did it.

Come down to the station on Monday.
Can't you just help me out now?

A little busy down here.
You a boxer, too?

Do I look like a fighter, kid?
That don't mean nothing. Look at those
clumsy fellas in the ring.

Palookas. The both of them. They got will, but no skill,
and they don't listen.
You their coach?

I'm coach and uncle. Teacher and counselor. I'm break-
ing muscles. They're chasing dreams.
Oh.

161

Most of these boys never gonna box for real, but at least
they get to knock out their anger in the ring, instead of
getting into trouble on the streets.
Where's your badge? You undercover?

Enough with the questions, I got to get back to work.
This is a cool place.

You know how to fight?
Never been beat up.

*That's not what I asked you. You a southpaw? How's your
jab? Show me an uppercut.*
. . .

If you wanna learn, come down here after school one day.
My momma won't allow that.

*Seems to me if you wanna whup somebody, you should
learn how to fight first.*
. . .

You know where I'll be.
But what about my bike?

*You can kiss that bike goodbye, kid, but we'll file that
report on Monday.*
Thanks. Hey, what's your name?

The sign on the door says Joe Martin's Gym, *and this is
my gym, so you can call me Joe Martin.*
Good to meet you, Joe Martin. I'm Cassius
Clay.

Momma, Please

let me go
down to the gym
to box, I begged.

I promise
I'll do better
in school,
even in French class,
plus I'll bring Rudy
and teach him,
and make sure
he doesn't get hurt.

The old man
said he would help me
find my bike, too,
and train me
to protect myself.
I've been born again, and
maybe I can be great
at something
besides my looks.

After Momma Bird finished
laughing, she agreed,
then told me
Cash was gonna buy me
a motor scooter
and that I better not
let that get stolen too.

I hooped and hollered.
Merci, I said, then hugged her
and ran to tell Riney
and Lucky the big news.

Cassius Clay is gonna be
a fighter.

ROUND SIX

As you've probably picked up by now, Cassius always thought big. Dreamed big. *Talked* big!

This one night when we were kids, we sat around his living room with Rudy and Mrs. Clay and listened to President Eisenhower on the radio. But even when a president was talking, Cassius would never shut up. He was too busy picturing *himself* in that big white mansion in Washington, D.C.

"I could be president!" he said. "I *should* be president!"

President Cassius Marcellus Clay Jr. He said that name would look good on money. Mrs. Clay just shook her head and tried to shush him, but Cassius would not quit.

"He's right," Mr. Clay added. "He would be the best president ever!"

"Not just the best; the most *beautiful* one!" Cassius said.

And I think he really, truly believed it.

I don't know what made him think that in a million years a black man could ever be president. In most places around where we lived, black people could hardly even *vote!* After a while, Cassius forgot about being president—but he stayed way too cocky about most other things.

Once, for about two weeks, all he talked about was the movie in his head where he beat Rocky Marciano —the undefeated heavyweight champion of the world! And in his movie, Cassius didn't just beat Marciano. He knocked him out! Cassius was the first man in history to KO the Rock from Brockton. In his dreams.

But sometimes, when it was just me and Cassius, that confidence slipped a little. It would dim and flicker. Call it nerves. Worry. Maybe fear of failing. Fear of not living up to his own movie. I remember when his first big fight was coming up, he acted all tough and flashy around most people. He bragged to Rudy. He shadowboxed rings around his daddy. He rolled up his sleeves, showing off his skinny arms, and pumped his biceps for Mrs. Clay. But sometimes, I could tell he was acting —putting on a show. Not just for them, but for himself, too. I think maybe it was his way of convincing himself of his own greatness.

I remember Cassius showing up at school in the morning with two raw eggs and a quart of milk. I watched him break the eggs into the milk, shake it all up, and drink the whole mess down in one long gulp.

"I'm the baaaaaaddest dude in Looville!" he'd shout, making sure that everybody could hear him. I guess he thought if everybody heard him, it kind of made it true.

Sometimes I saw Cassius get inspired by *real* movies. Every Saturday, we went to the Lyric, the Grand, or the Palace—the theaters down on Walnut Street. We saw every Western movie ever made. Every pirate movie. Every Tarzan movie. We wondered why the heroes in those movies were always white, even in the African jungle—but Cassius still loved seeing the good guy win in the end. Because that's how he wanted to see himself—a winner against all odds, no matter what.

The truth was, Cassius knew that most of the kids in the gym were bigger than he was. Maybe stronger. He knew there probably wouldn't be any headgear to protect him against those hard jabs and hooks. All around Joe Martin's gym, we saw old boxers with noses flattened like mashed turnips. Some of them had their ears all crushed and mangled too. Cauliflower ear, they called it.

169

"I don't wanna look like no vegetable, Lucky," said Cassius. "I gotta stay pretty."

And those boxing gloves. They were so dang heavy! Black leather, with "EVERLAST" in big letters around the wrists. When Cassius was starting out, those gloves felt like lead weights at the ends of his skinny arms, especially after a long training session or sparring match. One night when we were walking home, Cassius told me he was worried that he wouldn't be able to keep the gloves up in front of his face in a real fight. And if he let them drop, even for a second . . . *POW!* Turnip. Cauliflower.

They say fear is catching—and I admit that I caught a touch of it. I caught it from Cassius. I think deep down we both had the exact same fear—that when he finally did get to fight on TV, he would lose. And that his dream—his own personal movie— would end right then and there.

Distance

Me, Riney, and Lucky
go waaaaay back
like Cadillac seats,
since grade school,
but now Lucky goes
to a fancy Catholic school
for smart kids
on the other side
of town, so
I only see him
on weekends
or after school
when he comes by
the gym
to see me sparring.

Conversation with Lucky

How you like your school?
The food is nasty, but it's all right. They might
skip me a grade.

I wish I could skip the rest of 'em.
I think I might go to Bellarmine College and
study journalism.

To the Olympics is where I'm going. I'm too
slick for these tricks, Lucky.

You got to get past the Golden Gloves first,
Gee-Gee.

To win the Golden Gloves is my goal
and after that, it's Olympic Gold.
These fists of fury will be my claim to fame.
Kings and queens will know my name.
Say it loud, what's my name?

CASSIUS CLAY! ENOUGH YAPPING.
Oh, hey, Mr. Martin, I'm just funnin'.

Do that on your own time. This is my time.

Hey, Mr. Martin. Uh, I'll catch up with ya
later, Gee-Gee.

Later, Lucky.
Cassius, you got a dream?

Yes, sir, Mr. Martin, I'm gonna be a winner.
What's the best way to make a dream come true?

Only Way

to make a dream
come true
is to wake up.
You gotta put in
the work, Cassius,
Joe Martin growls
for the hundredth
or thousandth time
since the first day
I stepped foot
in his gym.

Cassius, jab jab cross,
jab jab cross,
and move your feet,
not your mouth
so much.

I don't know
why I can't
do both, I say, laughing
and jabbing.

Roadwork

Shuffle, backpedal,
skip, dash,
and roll.
That's half my training,
'cause Joe Martin says,
Boxers gotta run
so they don't get spent.
A fight is not a sprint,
it's like a short marathon, Clay!

So, I run
fast and slow,
alternating,
simulating
the rounds
in a ring,
to build up
my endurance,
keep my heart healthy,
get my lungs
and legs
strong enough
for the up

and the down
of each round
after round
after round.

Chickasaw Park

Most every day
we run before school,
take off quietly
out the back door
at 4:30 a.m. — me and Rudy
in our training gear:
green plastic trash bags draped
over us, and
heavy black paratrooper boots
that Lucky's security-guard uncle
brought us
from Fort Knox,
where he works.

We cut
straight through
Greenwood Cemetery,
zoom under the parkway
through the white neighborhoods
that we're supposed to stay out of
to get to Chickasaw,
where we run the park
three times,
circling the fishing pond,

the cluster of oak trees,
and the three tennis courts
that I nicknamed
FREE CLAY,
since they're the only clay courts
in Louisville
and ANYBODY can play there.

We race the last block
back to our house
as the sky dawns.
Rudy yawns,
hugs Momma—who's on
her way
to work—on the
front lawn,
then goes inside
to shower.

Hey, Bird.
I done told you I'm not one of your friends.

Sorry, Momma Bird, I say, still jogging in
place.
*I swear you so big, Gee-Gee, you done outgrown
your senses.*

Conversation with Bird

Anybody crazy enough to be up this early ain't got much
sense.
Suffer now, and live the rest of my life as a champ.

How long you gonna keep doing this, Gee-Gee?
Until I'm a beast in the east, and the best in
the west.

. . .

Bir — uh, Momma, I'm gonna be heavyweight
champion of the WORLD, and the first thing
I'm gonna do is buy you a big house up in
the Highlands just like the ones you clean for
them rich folks every day.

Son, don't mind my job, I don't. It's decent work.
My momma shouldn't be cleanin' toilets and
cooking food for nobody. Not for four dollars
a day. Not for nothing.

I take pride in my work, son. And God bless that four
dollars. It bought them trash bags you wasting.
I'm not wasting them. It's part of a fighter's
training, helps me sweat off the fat, keep my

weight right. Plus, I take pride too . . . in
being the Greatest.

Boxing doesn't make you the greatest.
Boxing's gonna take us away from all this.

We got a nice house, a car, food on the table, family.
The Bible says—
The Bible didn't get me and Rudy into
Fontaine Ferry Park, and it sho' ain't—

Boy, don't you dare blaspheme the Good Book.
I'm just saying, I don't need church to tell me
what I already know.

What you know and what you think you know is two
different things.
Momma, I know who I am, and whose I am.
That's what Granddaddy Herman told me.

God rest his soul.
. . .

You gonna have me late to work. Look after your brother,
make sure he's fresh. He likes to run water for thirty
seconds and call himself clean.

Okay, Momma.

And just promise me you gonna read your Bible, go to school, and at least try not to mess up your face doing that boxing.
I came in here pretty and I'm gonna leave here pretty.

Boy, you sillier than a goose.
Sweeter than juice, and stronger than Zeus, too.

182   *Bye, boy.*
Hold up, Momma. Been working on a poem for when I win the Olympics. Wanna hear it?

Hurry up and say it then, boy, 'fore I miss my bus . . .

My Victory Speech

The Olympics gave me quite the scare.
Fought three rounds with a big ol' bear.

Came at me all wild and frantic
with fists of fury from 'cross the Atlantic.

Threw a big left, then launched a right.
Exploded on me like dynamite.

But Cassius Clay did not retreat.
I knocked him into the ringside seats.

Yeah, he was strong, but I was stronger.
If you thought he'd win, you couldn't be
wronger.

Who's the boss that shook up the world?
Face so pretty, it's like a pearl.

I'm the greatest, you have been told.
Now, hand me my Olympic Gold.

Craps

After last period,
Me, Riney, Rudy,
and Big Head Paul
peep some of the older guys
shooting dice
behind the school,
so I pucker my lips
like I'm 'bout to
kiss Teenie or something,
then I sing

the word *New,*
Stretching it out — *NNNEEWWWWW!* — so
it sounds
like a police siren,
which makes
them jokers scram
so fast, they leave
all their coins
on the ground
for us
to run over
and snatch.

We Take

the free money,
then they head over
to Rainbow
for cheeseburgers
while I make my way
to the gym, chomping
on my second onion
of the day
'cause my father said
eating them raw
makes your bones stronger
and keeps you regular.

Regimen

Shadowboxing and jogging on Mondays.
Speed bags on Tuesdays.
Weightlifting on Wednesdays and Fridays.
Heavy bag on Thursdays.
Jumping rope and sparring on Saturdays
every week, but
Joe Martin doesn't think I'm ready,
still won't let me box
a proper fight
on *Tomorrow's Champions*.

Conversation with Joe Martin

When you gonna let me box on TV?
When you're ready, kid.

It's been almost a year. I'm ready now.
How many sit-ups you do today?

Four sets of fifteen.
When you do five sets of twenty and a hundred
lunges and you stop playing pranks, that's when.

You keep moving the finish line, how'm I supposed to
cross over? I'm ready.
I say when you're ready.

Just put me in the ring, and I'll show you. I'll win
every time.
The fight is won before you get in the ring.

What's that supposed to mean?
It means you gotta work harder, and faster, with
your body and your mind.

How'm I supposed to even get ready when you won't
let nobody hit me, Joe Martin?

Soon as you learn to keep your fists up and
protect your head.

Can't nobody catch me, so I don't need my fists up.
My feet protect me.
That's all fine, but some bruiser's gonna catch
you upside the head one day and you won't know
what hit you.

Not while I'm moving and grooving. I got music in
my soul, and rhythm in my sole. By the way, can we
get some Chuck Berry or Bo Diddley on in here?
You a dancer or a boxer?

Maybe I'm both. Cassius Clay, fists strong as iron, feet
fast as a lion.
Get back to your training . . . and keep your fists up.

So, when you gonna let me box on TV?
. . .

The First Time

Joe Martin
let me box,
it was
one round
with Caden Wilkinson,
a short sixteen-year-old
from the Highlands,
who pounded me
so hard
he bruised my jaw,
nearly broke my nose,
and woulda knocked me
out cold
if Joe Martin hadn't pulled me
out first.

Set your feet, Cassius. Angle your body. Move, and—
Yeah, I know, keep my fists up.

*You know it, then do it. Now go get some cotton so we
can clean that bloody nose.*

. . .

Sunday

I try to sneak
out the back door
to hit the gym,
but Bird catches me,
says, *Gee Gee, I told you*
no boxing
on the Sabbath, then sends
me and Rudy
to Aunt Coretta's house
so she can cut
our hair
before church.

I shadowbox
all the way
to Mount Zion Baptist,
then sit
in the back
of Sunday school
telling jokes
and showing off
my new card trick
until the teacher

offers five dollars to whomever

can recite

the most Bible verses.

Love

It's a tie
between Teenie
and Riney,
but he freezes
on the last word
and can't remember
the end of
And now these three remain:
faith, hope, and love.
But the greatest of these
is . . .

Teenie remembers,
we all clap for her,
and after she goes up
to get her five dollars,
doesn't even look
in my direction,
but blows Riney a kiss
that I hate to admit
makes me feel
some kind of way.

Conversation with Rudy

We're gonna be late for dinner.
We're not gonna be late.

How long we supposed to jump rope?
Till I say we finished, Rudy.

I know we supposed to train hard all the time, but it's
Daddy's birthday.
No birthdays or holidays for champions.

We not champions, though.
Yet. Starts in your mind, Rudy. Believe it,
achieve it. Heck, I'm already a champion. Call
me king of the swing.

How's about we call your brother the Louisville Lip.
Hey, Mr. Martin.

Hey there, Rudy.
That's funny. My brother, the Louisville Lip.

Y'all don't faze me.
What about Ronnie O'Keefe, he faze you?

Who's Ronnie O'Keefe?
The tall white boy in the ring over there.

Which one, Mr. Martin?
The one with that lightning-fast jab.

Nope, never heard of him. Doesn't look so fast to me.
*Well, you'll see for yourself, 'cause you're fighting
him Saturday night.*

I am?
He is?

194

Yup.
Where?

On TV.

Cassius Clay vs. Ronnie O'Keefe

NOVEMBER 12, 1954

We both come out
throwing blows
everywhichaway.

His arms long
and bony
as tree branches.

My feet wild like
the wind.
I blow by him

so fast, he can't lay
more than a few fingers
on me.

That's all you got? I whisper
in his ear
when he clinches into me

after a straight right punch
that misses my cheek
by an inch.

The ref separates us

and we go back at it,
mostly missing each other

until the end
of the second round
and most of the third,

when I land a series
of short pops
to his head,

one right below
his left ear
that makes him stumble

into the ropes
right in front of
where Cash and Rudy

and Lucky and my uncles
are sitting
and screaming,

KO! KO! KO!

but Ronnie gets saved
by the bell,

so I have to settle
for a split decision
and a four-dollar prize

in my debut fight.
Cassius Clay: One win.
    Zero losses.

Promotional Tour

To spread the word
about my next fight,
Cash said he would
drive me
around Louisville,
but he didn't come home
the night before,
and anyway
his truck was sitting
on two flats.

So I down a quart
of milk,
two raw eggs,
then take off
with Rudy and Riney
to knock on doors
and announce myself
to the world.

We walk through
black Parkland,
laughing
and cutting up

and telling everybody
how I'm gonna demolish
my next opponent
on TV.

Introducing Me

The name's Cassius Clay
and I'm gearing to fight.
My next foe may bark,
but I'm sure gon' bite!

If he comes in grinning
like he's having fun,
I'll wipe off that smile
and beat him in one.

If he tries to stick me
like Elmer's glue,
I'll turn up the heat
and sting him in two.

Tell all your friends
best bet on me
'cause ain't no way
he's lasting for three.

ROUND SEVEN

Want another scene from the movie starring Cassius?
Here's one. At least how I remember it:

It was a fall afternoon. We were out back at the
Clay house. Me, Cassius, and Rudy. We had borrowed
some of Mr. Clay's paints to make posters to promote
Cassius's next fight. But Cassius wasn't satisfied with
just names and places and dates and times. He had to
add a little drama. A little color. A little *poetry.*

Come see Clay go all the way, he wrote on one poster.
Another one said, *In just one round, his opponent goes
down.* I helped with the spelling. But the language was
all his. For Cassius, it wasn't enough to be a fighter. He
had to be a fighter with *flair.*

Cassius loved music. "Hound Dog" and "Long Tall
Sally" were on the radio all the time that year. I think
maybe that's where he got the ideas for his rhymes. He
always had songs in his head. But the words came out
pure Cassius.

By the end of the bout, his lights will be out! Like that.

After the paint dried, we hauled them all over the West End, putting up the posters wherever we could find an empty space on a wall or a fence.

We were putting up the last poster near a house on Virginia Avenue when we heard a screen door opening. A lady in a bright pink housecoat came out onto her stoop. She was looking straight at the poster—and she got red-hot mad.

"Hey! You boys can't put that poster up there!" she hollered.

"It's public property, ma'am," said Cassius. Polite as always. He put another tack through the poster.

"I know it is," the lady said, "but that's my *nephew* you're gonna be fighting. I can't have you bragging over him! Ain't *right!*"

Cassius looked at the poster. Right below his name (in smaller letters) was the name of his opponent. Jimmy Ellis.

"Ma'am?" Cassius asked, pointing at her. "You Jimmy's aunt?"

"That's right!" she said, pointing right back. "And I know who you are! You're Cassius Clay! And Jimmy is going to knock you silly!"

Cassius just smiled as he put the last tack in the poster. "Sorry, ma'am," said Cassius. "Jimmy and I are friends, but when we get into that ring, I don't know him. Nothin' silly about that." And at that very moment, I knew Jimmy Ellis was going down.

In Louisville, boxing for kids was so popular that they actually put it on television — on the local station WAVE. The show was called *Tomorrow's Champions*, and Cassius was the main attraction. In fact, he treated WAVE like his own personal TV empire. For every bout, he was so confident, it was like he'd already won before the fight even started. Cassius was just eighty-nine pounds when he licked his first opponent, Ronnie O'Keefe. And plenty more dropped after that. Big kids. Strong kids. When the bell rang, they came out swinging. Cassius just leaned back and let their punches land in midair. Then he started to jab back with his long arms.

Right! Left! Right! Left! *Thud! Thud! Thud! Thud!*

Pretty soon his opponents would be so tired from throwing air punches that they'd be bent over and panting!

Cassius was already at another level. He had a way of knowing exactly when a punch was coming and where it was coming from. "My built-in radar," he told me. Nobody—fans, trainers, sparring partners—had ever seen anything like it. "It can't be!" one ref said. But it was.

Pretty soon, my friend Cassius wasn't the only one saying he was the greatest. All over Louisville, everybody was saying the same thing.

Cassius Clay vs. James Davis

FEBRUARY 4, 1955

I won four fights
in a row,
one with a TKO,
so I took it a little easy
getting ready
for my big fight
in the Louisville Golden Gloves tournament
against a little
funny-looking
kid named
James Davis.

I slept in a lot,
skipped running
in Chickasaw
days at a time,
just ran to school
and back,
didn't drink much garlic water,
goofed around
with the fellas
at the gym,
stayed up late

reciting rhymes
with Rudy,
and ate almost
a whole chocolate cake
plus three bowls of ice cream
for dinner
on my 13th birthday
all of which is why
Joe Martin said
I looked sleepy,
fought with no killer instinct,
got beat

like a rented mule,
and lost my fifth fight
to a short,
funny-looking
kid named
James Davis.

Cassius Clay: Four wins.
One loss.

Cassius Clay vs. John Hampton

JULY 22, 1955

Hamp smiled when
he landed a few body
shots, so when he got

close enough to me
I whispered, That's all you got?
then threw a left jab

and a right hook that
sent him tumbling
to the mat.

Cassius Clay: Nine wins.
Two losses.

Conversation with Rudy

You racking up the wins, Gee-Gee. How do you feel?
I feel with my hands. Now let me practice.

I saw Teenie and Riney today.
I'm trying to concentrate, Rudy.

I'm just saying, I think they going together.
. . .

You know her cousin Alice?
Yeah.

She asked me to be her boyfriend.
I thought you already had a girlfriend, Rudy.

Just 'cause you don't have time for girls, Gee-Gee, don't mean I gotta be the same.
. . .

You think Riney and Teenie really a thing?
I DON'T KNOW, RUDY!

You mad?

Mad that you won't let me focus. Ain't nobody thinking about Riney, Teenie, or her cousin Alice. Now, unless you want a fat lip, you best let me finish my sit-ups.

Before

When we got home
from training
at the gym
I made Rudy jump rope
with me
for another fifteen minutes,
then do bicycle crunches
and sit-ups
in the backyard
until we both
just collapsed
under the stars, dreaming
about the future
until Cash brought us
back to the present.

We Thought

we'd done something wrong
when he kept hollering
for us to come inside,
but when we did
and saw him
shaking his head,
chin trembling,
and grief pouring
from his eyes,
we thought again.

And, when he showed us
the picture
of the dead boy,
we cried too.

I Was Thirteen

when I lost
my first fight,
and my first girl
to my best friend.

When Teenie told me
that she chose Riney
'cause I was married
to my boxing gloves
and the ring.

When I got real serious
about the sweet science,
trained and fought
like a madman.

When I decided
that one day
I was gonna become
the heavyweight champion
of the world.

When my daddy
showed us

a gruesome magazine photograph
of a twelve-year-old faceless boy
who was visiting family
in Mississippi
for the summer
when he was shot in the head,
drowned in the river,
and killed
for maybe whistling
at a white woman.

When I got to see
Emmett Till
and the face
of America.

After

Even though I won
the next few fights, I felt a
devastating loss.

I Was Thirteen

when I realized
that maybe boxing could
save us,
take me away
from all this.

The Next Few Years

I fought like a gladiator
ate like a champ
lit up contenders
in the ring like a lamp.

Sparred on the daily
kept my fists high
danced on my feet
like a black butterfly.

Me and Rudy Baker
battled two rounds
I sent him home crying
back to Smoketown.

Twice I laid
Donnie Hall out flat
walked all over him
like a doormat.

I boxed nonstop
and trained insane.
One thing on my mind:
NO PAIN, NO GAIN.

A Guy with a Camera

films me
dancing around
my corner,
waiting for the ref
to blow his whistle.

HEY, KID! another guy
in a baseball cap
with a pen
and pad yells
from the folded seats.
*YOU THINK YOU CAN TAKE JIMMY
ELLIS?*

I look
right square in the camera lens
and yell back . . .

Introduction: Reprise

I'll shake him, break him,
then take him out.

Who'll win this fight,
there should be no doubt.

Cassius Clay is unstoppable
and don't you forget

THE MAN TO BEAT ME
AIN'T BEEN BORN YET.

Cassius Clay vs. Jimmy Ellis
AUGUST 30, 1957

He came out smiling
and swinging,
strong and swift
like Duke Ellington
on the keys,
so I just danced
to the rhythm
in my head,
bobbing and weaving,
letting him tag me
a few times
so I could get a feel
for his might
for the fight
he was bringing,
and when I saw
he was getting tired
in the third
and final round
I whispered, No offense, Jimmy,
then smiled
for the cameras
and opened up

a can of Louisville blues
that he wasn't expecting
to hear.

I threw a solid punch
with my left
to his side
and while he was distracted
with the pain
I landed a quick, clean uppercut
with my right
to his jaw
that turned that smile
into a frown
and shut all his music off.

Cassius Clay: Sixteen wins.
Two losses.

Rematch

I saw Jimmy Ellis
at Fred Stoner's gym
and we got to talking
about the fight,
then some guys
started talking smack
about how
the judges did Jimmy wrong
and the fight was fixed
and whatnot,
so yeah, I told him
let's fight
again.

Cassius Clay vs. Jimmy Ellis, Part 2

More people in Louisville watched
our rematch than *I Love Lucy*
that week, which is good

'cause a million folks
saw my pretty face, but bad
'cause they saw it when

I took off my headgear
after losing in a split
decision: one judge

for me, and two for him.
Cassius Clay: Seventeen wins.
Three losses.

Conversation with Rudy

Sorry, Gee-Gee.
For what, Rudy?

I mean, 'cause of that last fight.
Can't have delight if you don't see the dark,
Rudy.

*Sound like something Granddaddy Herman would've
said.*
Rudy, I'm still the greatest. In fact, I may be
the double greatest.

Can I ask you a question, Gee-Gee?
I don't know, can ya?

Think we'll ever get there?
Get where?

The Golden Gloves?
Not if you don't quit interrupting my flow.

The kid who won this year was from Cleveland.

I know. He was a light middleweight. Strong,
though.

Not as strong as the kid a few years ago from St. Louis.
Never saw anybody hit that hard.
He was a heavyweight, Rudy. Name was
Sonny Liston.

I swear he hit so hard, Gee-Gee, he could probably turn
a human brain into grits.
Turn July into June.

That's one joker you don't wanna get in the ring with.
The fight is won before you get in the ring,
Rudy.

What's that supposed to mean?
Means I ain't gonna always be there to protect
you, so focus, Rudy.

I'm bigger than you, won almost as many fights as you.
What I need protection for?
Keep yapping, little brother, and I'll show
you.

Gee-Gee, can I ask you something?
You just did.

What we gonna do after high school?
Same thing we doing now. Knock out whoever's silly enough to get in the ring with us.

But that's not a job.
It was a job for Sugar Ray. And Joe Louis.

*I hear ya talking, Cassius, but maybe we ought
to have a backup. Like the army.*
I got two words for you and Uncle Sam.

What's that?
HECK and NO! Until this country treats
boys like me and you as human beings, I ain't
fightin' for no flag.

True.
Now, stop bothering me, and let me hit these
bags. I gotta be ready.

ROUND EIGHT

A boxer needs a ton of confidence — *way* more than normal people. How else could you step into a ring wearing nothing but shorts, shoes, and gloves, knowing the guy in the other corner would try like the devil to knock you out? Without confidence, you'd probably just turn around and run. I know *I* would!

Confidence is hard to understand. Hard to find. Hard to master.

There was one thing Cassius was *totally* confident about: He knew that boxing was the fastest way for a kid like him to become famous. So he made boxing his whole focus. Cassius was getting bigger and stronger, enough to play football or baseball or basketball. He probably could have won varsity letters in all three. But he focused on one thing and one thing only. Boxing was his way up and his way out. He just knew it.

Month after month, I sat against the wall at the Columbia Gym and did my homework while Cassius worked out. He was learning how to use his long arms and his quick feet—and I could see his confidence growing. Punch and move away. Pull back instead of duck. Stay out of the opponent's reach. Move fast. Hit hard. Stay pretty.

Even with all his skills and practice and focus, sometimes Cassius got knocked down. When it happened, he got madder at himself than at his opponent. But he knew that getting knocked down wasn't the worst thing.

"It's *staying* down that's wrong," he told me.

Cassius knew that to be the best, he had to learn from the best, no matter what it took. When we were in high school, the boxer Willie Pastrano came to town with his trainer, Angelo Dundee. Willie was a pro from New Orleans, and he had one of the most powerful left hands anybody had ever seen. I'll never know how, but Cassius found out which hotel Willie was staying in. He dragged me and Rudy downtown and led us right through the hotel lobby. Then he picked up a hotel phone and called Willie's room. I couldn't hear the other end of the conversation, only what Cassius said. After all these years, I can still recite it from memory:

"My name's Cassius Marcellus Clay. I'm the Golden Gloves champion of Louisville, Kentucky. I'm gonna win the National Golden Gloves, then the Olympics one day, and I want to talk to you."

It must have sounded like a prank call. I figured whoever was on the other end of the phone would just hang up. Instead, Cassius listened, put down the phone, walked across the lobby, and pressed the elevator button. As the elevator doors closed, he just smiled at us and said, "Wait here."

We waited for three hours.

When Cassius came back downstairs, it was like he had been pumped full of boxing juice. All the way home, he wouldn't stop talking about what Pastrano and Dundee had told him—about how a boxer should train, what to eat, how far to run, how much to hit the bag. It was a crash course in success, and Cassius soaked it up. Every word.

"Mr. Dundee said I was *a student of boxing*," said Cassius. On that day, I saw his confidence *glowing*.

Some people say the opposite of confidence is fear. Not me. I say it's *humility*. And for most people, that's the *last* word that comes to mind when they think of Cassius Clay. He was loud. He was proud. He called himself the Greatest. Even when he wasn't. Yet. But deep down, where it mattered, he could be very humble. It was another part of him that he didn't let most people see.

I could tell that it bothered him that his mother got only four dollars a day for working dawn to dusk.

Cassius made that much from just one bout on local TV. He told me that one morning, when his momma was waiting for the bus on her way to her cleaning job, he walked up and stood next to her.

"Where you think you're going?" she asked.

"I'm going to work," said Cassius, "with *you.*"

She tried to shoo Cassius home, but he just stood there. When the bus came, they got on together, moved to the back like always, and rode to a white neighborhood across town—a place where the only black people were the ones carrying mops, buckets, and brooms.

For that whole day, Cassius was on his hands and knees with his mother—polishing floors, cleaning toilets, wiping down furniture. When Mrs. Clay paused at the door before they left, she had to admit the house never looked better. Cassius put his big hand on her shoulder as they walked back to the bus. Not many people could make Cassius Clay feel humble. But his mother did. Every day.

Birthday

For my birthday
Rudy gave me
the silver dollar
Granddaddy Herman had given him
for Christmas
when we were little.

Papa Cash and Momma Bird gave me
Elite Everlast boxing gloves
with cushions
soft as a cloud
and my name
painted on them.

And Lucky gave me
a magazine
that had a boxing story
called "Fifty Grand"
by a writer
named Ernest Hemingway,
who I'd heard about
in Mrs. Lauderdale's class.

We read some of it,
but I decided
I didn't like it
'cause any white fella
who calls a black person
by *that name*
don't deserve
to be read.

Beat

By the time I finally made it
to Chicago
for the 1958 National Golden Gloves
championships,
I'd been fighting
for almost five years,
showed my talents
on *Tomorrow's Champions*
seven times,
and won

more than thirty fights,
ten by knockout.

But none of that mattered,
since Cash
wasn't screamin'
my name ringside
for the first time ever,
because he'd gotten
into a dustup
before I left
that ended
with the cops
on our doorsteps.

I won the first two
and lost the finals
Because you didn't keep your fists up,
and you didn't get out of the way.
You let him hit you too much, Joe Martin
told me after the fight,
and he was probably right,
but also because
the few times
I had a little rally going
I couldn't get
into a rhythm
'cause it seemed like
there was nobody
in the whole arena
singing my name.

Cassius Clay vs. Kent Green

FEBRUARY 26, 1958

The newspaper article said:

The sixteen-year-old pugilist
from Louisville
with quick feet
and a loud mouth
showed promise
in his first two fights
but got outboxed
in the semifinals
by the older, more seasoned,
hard-punching
Kent Green,
who targeted
the younger Clay
like a lion
stalking
a gazelle,
then unloaded
enough head shots
for the ref
to stop the fight

in round two
of the National Golden Gloves semifinals.

Cassius Clay: Eighteen wins.
Five losses.

Lucky Read

the article
to himself
on my front porch
while I shadowboxed
with Riney
and skipped rope
on the lawn.

Me and Riney
hadn't really hung out much
since he and Teenie
got serious, but she was
visiting relatives
in Nashville,
so we were yapping
and catching up
when my momma
told us to go pick up
her order
from Leonard's grocery store.

We were walking home
with *beaucoup* bags
of food and stuff,

which I didn't mind
'cause I was working out
the muscles
in my arms,
but they hated
'cause Momma Bird bought
the whole store,
which was twelve blocks away.

I'd rather starve, Gee-Gee, Riney said,
than carry all these heavy bags,
when someone started
screaming
my name
from behind us.

Face-Off

The three of us
turn around
and see
some suspicious-looking Smoketown fellas
approaching us
like they got something bad
on their minds.

Leading their gang,
smack-dab in the front
is a meaner
and taller-looking Tall Bubba,
whose face is still not back
to normal,
and right beside him
is his new best friend,
Corky Butler.

Conversation with Corky Butler

You been dodging me, Cassius?
. . .

*Fellas, Cassius Clay been avoiding the undisputed cham-
pion of the streets, but time done caught up with him.
What you want, Chalk—Corky?* Riney says,
wishing he hadn't.

*What I want is y'all off my block, but you here, and you
know what that means. Pay the toll!*
This not your block, Lucky answers, like he got
fists to back it up.

If I'm on it, it's my block.
. . .

A quarter a head. It's three of you, so that's one dollar.
Three of us, Lucky says, *is seventy-five cents.*

*Interest and tax is a quarter, fool. Pay me my four
quarters.*
We don't have four quarters, I say.

Then you gotta part with one of them bags.
I'm not giving you my momma's groceries.

*Then I'm gonna lay you out like you got laid out at them
Golden Gloves,* he says, laughing.
. . .

*Hey, fellas, who got thumped real bad by big Kent
Green?*
They all start chanting, *CASSIUS! CASSIUS!
CASSIUS!*

*Oh, I'm just messin'. Can't fight ya today, we meeting
some girls at the movies. I'll catcha another time. Gimme
five on that,* he adds, laughing, then holding out his
palm for me to slap it.
I can't give you five, 'cause you full of jive . . .

Sometimes My Mouth Moves Faster Than My Mind

I'd give you eight,
but ya teeth ain't straight.

This makes some of his gang giggle,
but it's the next thing I say

that has them all laughing
out loud like hyenas

and brings me face-to-face
with the wrath of Chalky.

I would give you thirty
but your face too dirty.

Can't give you forty, 'cause—
You got a big lip, Clay, Corky says,

taking a swing
that I dodge,

just as a police car creeps by,
eyeing us all.

How about I make it a big FAT one!
How about you try? I say back.

I should knock you out
right here, but I want

the whole world to see
these fists upside your head.

Name the day and the time, Corky.
Me and you in the ring.

Then let's do that.
Then let's do that.

You're Crazy

if you get in the ring
with him, Riney says,
as we pick up the bags

and turn to leave.
Yeah, Gee-Gee,
he doesn't fight fair, Lucky chimes in.

He's liable to have
some rocks
in his gloves, and

I knew they were both right
and for a quick second
I was beginning to have

second thoughts
about boxing him,
until I heard Corky Butler yell

from halfway down the block,
HEY, CASSIUS, IS THIS YOURS?
then launch toward me

the purple lucky rabbit-foot key chain
that Teenie had hooked
to the spotlight clamp

on the handlebars
of my stolen, brand-new
red Schwinn bicycle.

Cassius Clay vs. Corky Butler

JULY 26, 1958

Corky was shorter
than me
but I swear he looked
like what a giant earthquake
would look like
if it boxed
and planned
on killing someone.

I bounced
on my side of the ring,
shuffled my feet,
smiled for the crowd,
recited the Lord's Prayer,
anything to hide my shaky knees
and the fact
that I was scared
to death.

Behind my corner
was Cash bragging,
Bird, with her eyes closed
like she did at most

of my fights,
my brother
plus all the cats
from the neighborhood,
and some classmates
standing ringside,
cheering me on.

The bell rang
and I came out throwing jabs,
quickly moving
out of the way

of his mile-a-minute sledgehammer punches
'cause if just one of them landed
I'd have been out
for the count.

In the second round,
he musta swung
fifty times, but
couldn't connect
'cause he couldn't catch me,
plus he started getting tired,
and a little slower.
He chased me
around the outdoor ring

and each time
he got close enough
I just ducked,
tagged him real good,
and kept moving.

Then, outta nowhere,
he quit.

That's right.
Before the end
of the second round

of our showdown,
Corky Butler,
the baddest bully in Louisville,
screamed, *This ain't fair,* then
ran out of the ring
with a black eye
and a bloodied ego.

ROUND NINE

Sometimes, I think I knew Cassius better than I knew myself. I could tell that all the seeds of his greatness were already in him back in Louisville. He was bound for big things. I knew it. A lot of people did.

Unless you were around him back then, it's hard to imagine his dedication to boxing—his preparation, his focus. When he was getting ready for the National Golden Gloves competition, Rudy and I trained with him every single day. We ran with him, jumped rope with him, shadowboxed with him. Naturally, he left us in the dust. And after we were both worn out, Cassius just kept going.

But there were times when Cassius wore even *himself* out. Like the time he fell asleep in the Nazareth College library. I know what you're thinking—a library is the last place you'd expect to find Cassius. But he wasn't there to read. It was his night job. For sixty cents an hour, he dusted the shelves and waxed the tables and chairs. No doubt he learned how by watching his mother clean houses. But one night he was so exhausted from training that he just put his head down on one of the tables and drifted off. Funny, there's a sign in that library, still today, that says, *Cassius slept here.*

As the trip to Chicago got closer and closer, Cassius kept his eye on that Golden Gloves championship. Along the way, he'd gotten knocked to the mat a few times, but you could never *keep* him down. That's a lesson I learned from Cassius—and I hold it close to this very day. My idea was always to be a writer. And believe me, I've had my share of rejections and failures. But I always got back up—just like Cassius taught me—and kept on writing.

In June, I sat with the Clay family when Cassius graduated from Central High School. Some of the teachers had said Cassius shouldn't get his diploma because he hadn't passed English. He still owed Mrs. Lauderdale a term paper. But the principal, Mr. Wilson, was in Cassius's corner. He said to the teachers, "One day our greatest claim to fame is going to be that we knew Cassius Clay, or taught him." So Mrs. Lauderdale told Cassius he could give an oral presentation instead of writing a paper. It didn't come as much of a shock that Cassius decided to talk about his adventures as an amateur boxer. He made Rudy and me sit on his front porch while he practiced that speech over and over—and got better each time. We all knew Cassius wasn't a great writer. But he was a world-class talker. And of course, he passed.

When they called his name at graduation, Cassius got a standing ovation. You couldn't hear yourself with how loud that applause was. That got Mrs. Clay crying. After the ceremony, Cassius hugged her for a solid five minutes. He was always a good son, a good brother, a good friend.

Years later, after one of his historic fights, a big-time sports reporter asked him what he wanted to be remembered for. This is what he said:

"I'd like for them to say, he took a few cups of love, he took one tablespoon of patience, one teaspoon of generosity, one pint of kindness. He took one quart of laughter, one pinch of concern, and then he mixed willingness with happiness, he added lots of faith, and he stirred it up well. Then he spread it over a span of a lifetime, and he served it to each and every deserving person he met."

I make my living as a writer. I wish I'd written that.

So, what about that Golden Gloves championship fight in Chicago? What do you think happened? Did

Cassius get knocked down one more time? I'll never forget that night. I saw it all, live, from the front row.

The way I see it, that's the night everything really began. The night it all got real.

At Central High School

I got sent
to Mr. Wilson's office
a lot

for talking
in Miz Raymond's class
while she read *Invisible Man*

for keeping raw onions
and garlic
in my pockets

for trashing
the devil's food cake
she brought in
for her birthday
and asking her why
did angel food cake
get to be white

for drawing a portrait
of her
without her wig

for not doing the homework
'cause I was too busy
training at Columbia Gym
from four o'clock till eight
and sparring at Fred Stoner's gym
from eight till midnight

for daydreaming
about what combinations
I was gonna throw
at the Golden Gloves:

Jab

        Step

to the left

        Duck

Step

        to the right

for not wanting
to be
invisible.

The Principal

Clay, you have a unique set of gifts.
I do believe you
will one day be
a boxing champion, he'd say,
but if you're gonna make it
out of high school,
I'm gonna need you
to get your mind right.

Then he'd give me
a history lesson,
like Granddaddy Herman used to.

You know, a lot of people sacrificed
for you to be exceptional, Cassius.
If you're gonna be the greatest,
best to start acting like it.

Then he'd start reading
Invisible Man
or whatever book
we were reading,

picking up
where Miz Raymond left off.

And I'd listen.

Talking Trash

It's hotter
than a Texas parking lot
in this joint,
yelled a burly fella
who was also training
for the '59 National Golden Gloves.

This hot ain't squat, Mr. Big Shot,
I hollered back, still hitting
the speed bags.

These fists I got are meteors,
super-hot,
burn you up like kilowatts,
knock you outta this world
like an astronaut.

Cassius, you a lightweight.
You don't want
no parts of me, he growled
from the ropes.
You may have scared
that nasty Corky fella, but
you don't scare me.

I'm a real monster.
I'm King Kong,
and I'll tear ya limbs off,
stick 'em in that running mouth
of yours.

You right about King Kong, I shot back,
'cause you one big, ugly sucker,
and I don't want
no parts of that ugly.

The place went ape crazy,
laughing with me,
at him.
He came out of the ring,
charging like a bull,
till one of his trainers
cut him off,
called him *CHAMP,*
then told me,
Loose lips sink ships.

I don't care if he is
a heavyweight, I hollered.
Tell that CHUMP

Cassius Clay don't panic,
I'll take him down
just like the *Titanic*.

After Winning

my second Louisville tournament trophy,
Joe Martin told me
I was ready
for Chicago again,
for the National Golden Gloves,
said I was moving
like a mustang,
finally keeping
my head
and my fists up,
throwing jabs
swift and easy,
and that I should
take a day off,
rest my body,
give my mind a workout,
before the trip,
so he sent me
to the YMCA
to watch fight films
and study the greats.

Cassius, immature boxers imitate,
mature boxers steal, he said, laughing.

So that's what I did.

Jack Johnson vs. Tommy Burns

DECEMBER 26, 1908

John Arthur "Jack" Johnson,

aka the Galveston Giant,

was big and strappy,

a hard-as-coal brute

who knocked out everybody

he fought, except

Tommy Burns, the heavyweight champion,

who refused to fight him,

until Johnson chased

and stalked him

around the world

for nearly two years,

buying ringside seats

to his fights

just to heckle

and hound him

into the ring.

For fourteen rounds,

I watched the Goliath Johnson

toy with Burns like

he was David

without a slingshot.

In the first couple minutes
of each round,
Johnson taunted him,
laughing at Burns's blows,
sometimes even making jokes
to the fans sitting
ringside,
and at the end
of each round
he'd punish Burns
with a barrage
of powerful punches
that over time
just crushed him.

I never got to see
round 15,
and neither did
the 2,000 people
standing
inside Sydney Stadium
in Australia,
'cause Johnson lifted Burns
off his feet
with an uppercut
that demolished him

so handily,

the local police

turned off the film cameras,

rushed into the ring,

stopped the fight,

all so no one ever got to see

John Arthur "Jack" Johnson,

aka the Galveston Giant,

become

the first black

heavyweight champion

of the world.

The Brown Bomber

Granddaddy Herman
and Papa Cash
used to argue
over everything — from
whether it was gonna rain
that day to
who got to eat
the last piece
of fried chicken — but
the one thing
they never disagreed on
was the best
heavyweight boxer
in history.

Joe Louis Barrow,
aka the Brown Bomber
from Detroit,
wasn't flashy,
stayed pretty quiet
in and out
of the ring,
but boxed loud,
fought with short,

powerful counterblows
like Jack Johnson, only
his were faster,
more precise combinations.

He let his fists
do the talking,
and boy did they HOLLER.

Louis had a right cross
that could probably level
Superman.
One punch
was all he needed
but he always threw
a flurry, battering each
of his 51 opponents
in knockouts
as heavyweight champion
until he met
the BROCKTON Bomber.

Joe Louis vs. Rocky Marciano
OCTOBER 26, 1951

Rocky was four inches shorter,

looked up

to Joe Louis

as a god,

but when they got

into the ring,

it was just two mortals—one young,

one aging—going at it.

The match was brutal.

I only watched

it once

'cause who really wants

to see

their hero

get older,

get slower,

get knocked

off their pedestal

by the new guy.

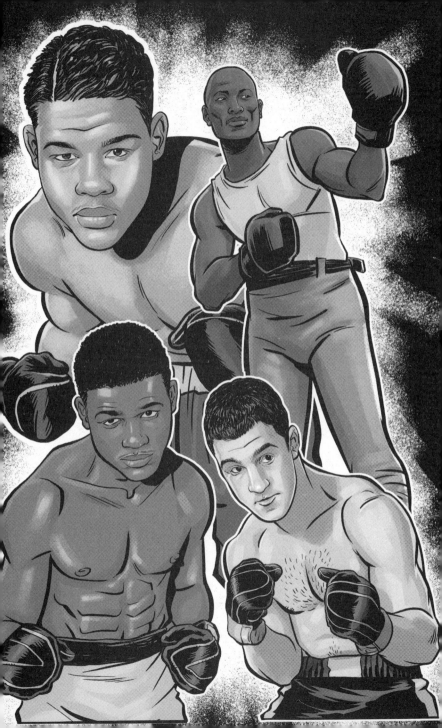

Rocky was a swarmer,
a slugger,
and a brawler
who liked to crouch
and strike
from down under,
which he did
against Louis
for eight long rounds,
and it wasn't pretty.

The next morning,
a sports reporter wrote
in the *New York Herald Tribune:*

Rocky hit Joe
a left hook
and knocked him down.
Then Rocky hit him
another hook
and knocked him out.
A third and final blow
to the neck followed
that knocked him
out of the ring.

And out of
the fight business.

That was Joe Louis's last fight
and probably the biggest
of Rocky Marciano's
record-breaking
49–0 career
as a professional boxer.

Sweet as Sugar

While I wait
for the front-desk clerk
at the YMCA
to load
the Sugar Ray Robinson
highlight film,
Lucky reads out loud
from a biography
we checked out
of the library.

Walker Smith Jr.
was fifteen
when he changed
his name,
when he borrowed
his older friend
Ray Robinson's birth certificate
so he could box
in a tournament
for boys eighteen
and older.

When the film starts,

we watch

in awe

as Sugar Ray dances

around the ring,

destroying

fighter after fighter

with a sweet, deadly

knockout left hook

that wipes the mat

with his opponents

one hundred and seventy-three times,

almost half of them

before the first round

even ends.

I'm gonna slay like Sugar Ray, I say,

jumping up,

mimicking

his fancy footwork

and sharp jabs.

Bon Voyage

Momma throws me
a party fit
for a king,
but won't let
me, Rudy, Lucky,
Riney, Small Bubba,
and Big Head Paul
eat till all my aunts, uncles,
and cousins show up,
and Cash gets back
from Aunt Coretta's
with the desserts.

Finally, he blows the horn
for me to come out
and help him
bring in the cakes,
and when I do
I run smack-dab
into Teenie Clark.

Conversation with Teenie

Hey, Teenie.
Hey, Gee-Gee.

You looking for Riney?
I'm looking for you.

I'm kinda in the middle of preparing for the Chicago
Golden Gloves tournament.
I heard. That's why I came.

. . .
Just wanted to say good luck, Cassius Clay.

Okay, thank you.
Why you acting so weird?

I'm not acting weird.
You still have that rabbit foot I gave you?

Yep. But, I don't need no luck. The fighter ain't been
born to beat me.
Well, you better not lose, then.

. . .

. . .

How's your new school?
Every student gets a book, and each class has its own pair of scissors.

Sounds decent.
Yeah, it is, but the white boys are daft.

I don't know what that means.
It means they're stupid. And sometimes mean. Integration is not so nice.

I thought the Supreme Court said integration was gonna solve all the problems.
They lied. Going to school with white boys liable to cause more problems.

True.
You having a party?

It's not really a party.
You gonna invite me in, Gee-Gee?

. . .

Sure smells good in there.

You can come in if you want. Riney's inside.
Why, thank you, Gee-Gee. Don't mind if I do.

Golden Gloves Party Menu

Three trays of meatloaf
Two bowls of cornbread dressing
Two huge buckets of fried chicken
A huge pot of collard greens
A ham hock
A macaroni casserole
Dozens of hot buttered rolls
Two large strawberry sheet cakes
Boatloads of strawberry ice cream
And a great big ol' pitcher
of extra-sweet tea.

Momma Bird's Prayer

We gather together
to send this boy out
into the world,
and ask that you hold
his dreams tight,
let them rocket
to the stars
and beyond.
Life is like a sky
full of possibility
and Gee-Gee is our
great golden eagle.

In this room full of angels,
remember whose you are, Cassius Clay.
Hold fast!
Together, we can dream a new world.
United we stand,
divided we fall—

GOD BLESS US, Cash interrupts. *NOW, LET'S EAT,*
Y'ALL!

After Dinner

Cash is drinking, laughing, and hugging on Bird.
Lucky's reading *Lord of the Flies,* not saying a word.

Riney and Teenie on the couch eating cake,
and Rudy ate so much he's got a bellyache.

All my cousins congratulate me.
Aunts and uncles celebrate me.

Bird says, *Show 'em your appreciation,*
so I put on a magical demonstration.

Pick a Card

and remember it,

then place it

back in the deck, I say to Riney,

winking at Teenie,

while shuffling

the cards

and recounting the story

about that time

Cobb and Jake were walking to school

in the blizzard

and they slid

down the hill

on Virginia Avenue,

got trapped

beneath the snow,

and how I was running by

and heard them screaming,

then dug 'em out

with my big paratrooper boot.

When I finish,

I spread the whole deck

face-up

on the table,
but one card is face-down.
Turn it over, I say,
and he does.

How'd You Do That?

Riney asks,
on my front porch
waiting for Teenie
to say goodbye
to everybody
in my family.

It's just science, y'all, Big Head Paul says.
Ya know Gee-Gee got a memory like a hawk,
Rudy chimes in.

All y'all wrong.
It's misdirection.
I get you to commit
to believing
in me
before I even show you
the card trick.
Your expectations
and my reality
all mixed up together.
I knew your card
before you knew it.

*That ain't even possible, Gee-Gee. Plus, you shuffled
them all out of order,* Lucky says.

Or, I shuffled them IN order
and created chaos
in your mind.

Huh? Rudy asks, scratching his head.
*What did the story about digging Cobb out of
the snow have to do with it, though?* Riney asks.

I told you, it's misdirection. I get you thinking what
I want you to think, then I can get you to do what I
want you to do.
Y'all talking about boxing again? Teenie asks,
coming out the front door.

Yep, I think. That's exactly what I'm talking about.
*I sure hope you knock some cans off at the
Golden Gloves, Gee-Gee,* Lucky says, giving
me five before he leaves.

Yeah, win it for the West End, for Louisville, Big Head
Paul says, waving goodbye.

Good luck at the tournament, Gee-Gee, Riney
says, shaking his head as he and Teenie leave
hand in hand.

He doesn't need luck, right, Cassius? Teenie hollers back.
Sure don't, I yell. Fight is won way before you
get in the ring.

The Night Before

I leave
for the finals
of the 1959 Golden Gloves
Tournament of Champions
in Chicago
I sprint through Chickasaw Park,
then down by
the Ohio River,
shadowbox
the frigid nighttime air,
get my head right,
think about
my future.

On the way back
I jog through
Bellarmine College
in the Highlands,
where Lucky says
he's gonna go,
pass by
Columbia Auditorium & Gym,

then decide to

run through Greenwood Cemetery

and visit with

my past.

Amen. Amen. Amen.

Granddaddy Herman
Because of you
I know who I am
I know whose I am and
I know where I'm going
I hope you can see that
Your words changed me
And I remembered
You told me
I am the greatest

Not because I am better than anybody
I am the greatest
Because nobody is greater than me
I'm going to win the Golden Gloves
Even though I'm the underdog
I been training my body and my mind and
Tomorrow's the real beginning for me
I guess I just wanted to say thank you and
that
Even though I haven't been back here since
the funeral,
I think about you all the time and
I love you, Granddaddy Herman.

The Day Of

I slip on my white Everlast shorts
lace up my black boxing boots
get taped up, my hands
placed firmly
inside the gloves,
then walk out
into the loud
and massive
Chicago Stadium
holding my history
in one hand
and my cool
in the other.

Cassius Clay vs. Tony Madigan

MARCH 25, 1959

Tony was an Aussie
with wild, stringy hair
sitting on top
of a block head
that housed
a chin
made of brick,
which didn't even flinch
at the jabs
I landed, but
by the middle
of the third round
I could tell
he was getting tired
of chasing me
around the ring,
of me dodging
his punches,
so I moved quicker
punched harder
and even though
he got me
into the corner,

pummeled me
with body shots,
I was too slick for tricks,
had a swift uppercut
with his name on it
that made him wince.
And I talked trash
the whole time,
told him if he even dreamed
he was gonna beat me,
he better wake up
and apologize.

Tony Madigan didn't stand a chance
'cause I was fighting
for my name
for my life
for Papa Cash
and Momma Bird
for my granddaddy
and his granddaddy
for Miz Alberta
for Riney and Teenie
for Big Head Paul
for Rudy
even for Corky Butler

for Louisville
for America
for my chance
for my children
and their children
for a chance
at something better
at something way
greater.

FINAL ROUND

Knowing Cassius Clay made me feel like I was a little part of history. We all felt that way. Of course, Cassius felt like he was a much *bigger* part of history. And he was so right!

After losing in Chicago in 1958 to Kent Green, Cassius went on to win not just one, but *two* Golden Gloves championships, then the Gold Medal at the 1960 Olympics. After that, he turned pro—which meant he started to make a *lot* more than four dollars a fight! His first professional bout was right in our hometown of Louisville. I was there—along with Rudy and a bunch of the guys we grew up with. Cassius won that fight, just like he won his next *nineteen* fights. For the next three years, he never lost in the ring. Not once.

In 1964, when he was just twenty-two, Cassius fought the heavyweight champion Sonny Liston, the Big Bear. People said Liston was *unbeatable*. But Cassius had a plan, and he made sure everybody knew it before he stepped into the ring. "Float like a butterfly, sting like a bee!" he said. And that's exactly what he did. Sonny Liston was older and more experienced—but he'd never experienced anything like Cassius Clay! When the seventh-round bell rang, Liston just sat there. He was done. And Cassius was king. The heavyweight champion of the world. Just like he'd predicted. Just like we'd all believed.

With all his success, Cassius never stopped thinking about unfairness and injustice—the way black people were looked down on in Louisville and everywhere he traveled. The day after the Liston fight, Cassius announced that he had joined the Nation of Islam—a movement that was founded to give black people a new sense of pride. A week later, he changed his name to Muhammad Ali. He said that he now thought of Cassius Clay as his "slave name." From that day on, I never called him Cassius again. (He still called me Lucky, though.)

In 1965, Ali beat Sonny Liston again. First-round knockout. Six months later, he beat Floyd Patterson. Ali was on top of the world and at the top of his game. Nothing could stop him—except a single sheet of paper.

In early 1967, Ali received a draft notice that ordered him to go into the army. That meant he would have to put on a uniform, carry a gun, and probably go

to war. But Ali did not believe in war. It was one thing to fight another man in a boxing ring — but the idea of killing people in a far-off country was not in Ali's nature. He didn't consider those people his enemies. He had no quarrel with them, he said.

So when the day came for Ali to step forward and enlist, he just refused. To this day, some people say it was a *brave* thing to do, and some say it was the *wrong* thing to do. But, knowing Ali, I realized that it was the *only* thing to do — even though we both understood that it might be the end of his boxing career. It almost was.

Officials took away Ali's heavyweight boxing title and his boxing license. He didn't box again for over three years — a time when he could have defeated more opponents and made millions of dollars. But his *beliefs* were what mattered most to him. He took those years to focus on black pride and racial justice. And he began to realize that there were more important things in life than boxing.

In 1970, after a long legal battle, Ali won his license back, which meant he could finally box again. His first opponent was Jerry Quarry, one of the toughest pros in the world. We all worried that Ali might be rusty after not boxing for so long. And he was — a little. But even a rusty Ali was better than most fighters in their prime

—and *definitely* better than Jerry Quarry. Ali won the fight in under three rounds.

Five months later, Ali took on "Smokin' Joe" Frazier. And lost! It was his first defeat as a pro. But Ali wasn't ready to give up—not by a long shot. In fact, he wanted a rematch with Frazier. Which he got. Which he won, and regained the heavyweight championship title.

In 1974, Ali fought the reigning champ George Foreman, who had never lost in forty-three pro fights. The bout was held in Africa, so they called it the Rumble in the Jungle! For this fight, Ali came up with a new strategy he called rope-a-dope. He cushioned his body against the elastic ropes around the ring so Foreman's punches wouldn't land as hard. By that time, I was writing for a big newspaper, so I was right there ringside for the fight. I'll never forget it! Ali won by a knockout in the eighth round.

In 1975, Ali fought Joe Frazier for a third time— this time in the Philippines. It was called the Thrilla in Manila. The fight went on for fourteen rounds, and at the end, Ali was the winner. A billion people around the world watched that fight on TV. A *billion!* Pretty cool.

I knew Ali couldn't go on winning forever, but the end came sooner than I thought it would.

He lost his next two fights, in 1980 and 1981. They turned out to be the last fights of his career. Outside the ring, I had started to notice a little trembling in his hands, and sometimes he couldn't form sentences clearly. We both knew something was wrong. Doctors told Ali he had Parkinson's disease, which affects muscles and body movement—and it was only going to get worse.

That news would have stopped most men. But not Ali. He never boxed again, but he kept on fighting. He fought to raise money for famine victims all over the world. He fought to get fifteen American hostages released from Iraq. He became friends with Michael J. Fox, a popular young actor who had Parkinson's disease too. Together, they raised millions of dollars for medical research. Ali worked with the United Nations and became a messenger for peace. In 2005, President Bush awarded him the Presidential Medal of Freedom. Ali told me that was one of his proudest days.

Muhammad Ali died in Arizona in 2016. I wasn't there. And in a way, I'm glad. Because I wouldn't want to remember him that way—still and quiet. I want to remember him as the funniest kid in the West End of Louisville—the kid who never stopped running and never stopped talking. Muhammad Ali was a three-time heavyweight champion of the world, and one of the most famous and respected men who ever lived.

He was also a true and loyal friend. That's what I'll remember most.

BIBLIOGRAPHY

Ali, Hana. *At Home with Muhammad Ali: A Memoir of Love, Loss, and Forgiveness.* New York: Amistad/Harper Collins, 2019.

Ali, Muhammad. *The Greatest: My Own Story.* New York: Random House, 1975.

———. Muhammad Ali Oral History Project tapes. Louisville, KY: Muhammad Ali Center.

Clark, Norman. *All in the Game: Memoirs of the Ring and Other Sporting Experiences.* London: Methuen, 1935.

Denenberg, Barry. *Ali: An American Champion.* New York: Simon and Schuster, 2014.

Early, Gerald, ed. *The Cambridge Companion to Boxing.* Cambridge, UK: Cambridge University Press, 2019.

Eig, Jonathan. *Ali: A Life.* Boston: Houghton Mifflin Harcourt, 2017.

Kimball, George, and John Schulian, eds. *At the Fights: American Writers on Boxing.* New York: Library of America, 2011.

Parkinson, Michael. *Muhammad Ali: A Memoir.* UK: Hodder & Stoughton, 2018.

Reed, Ishmael. *The Complete Muhammad Ali*. Quebec: Baraka Books, 2015.

Rotella, Carlo, and Michael Ezra, eds. *The Bittersweet Science: Fifteen Writers in the Gym, in the Corner, and at Ringside*. Chicago: University of Chicago Press, 2017.

ACKNOWLEDGMENTS

For her unflappable enthusiasm and candor, I thank, first and foremost, Lonnie Ali; without her permission and support, this book about her husband would not be. For access to some very essential, never-before-published oral histories, I thank Donald E. Lassere, Casey Harden, and the Muhammad Ali Center in Louisville, Kentucky. For his boundless insight, I am indebted to Ali's friend and associate Bernie Yuman. For being early readers of the manuscript (and listeners to part of it), I thank Beatrice Saba, Randy Preston, Van Garrett, Stephanie Stanley, and Samayah Alexander (who allowed her father to cut short several card games so that he could get back to writing). I am grateful to Jonathan Eig for the brief conversation about Ali that served as early inspiration. I thank Arielle Eckstut and Margaret Raymo, the bookends to my shelf of ideas, two inspiring examples of vision and calm in pursuit of our common literary interests. For his illustrative swagger, I thank our brilliant artist, Dawud Anyabwile. Jim

Patterson, many, many thanks for asking me, for trusting this collaboration. And *cheers* to Lois Cahall, my ebullient friend, who brought Jim and I together.

To my father, thank you for regularly requiring me to clean our garage, where I first discovered Muhammad Ali's autobiography in a crate of books. And a final thank-you to the American School in London, where I wrote most of this novel, and the countless coffee and tea houses around the city, where I ruminated on this story and buttermilk scones.

Kwame Alexander

310   The Muhammad Ali Estate would like to thank Lonnie Ali, Jamie Salter, Nick Woodhouse, Corey Salter, Marc Rosen (for Lex and Teddy), Katie Jones, Jim Gibb, Andrew Miller, Rick Richter, and Jennifer Gates.